COPYCAT
MURDERS

T.H. HUNTER

COPYCAT MURDERS is the third book in the COZY
CONUNDRUMS series.

CONTENTS

CHAPTER 1

Judge Immanuel Robinson raised a white handkerchief to his forehead, wiping away the ever-present drops of perspiration that had plagued him since the beginning of the trial in early June of that year. Despite the crowded courtroom, a makeshift construction in the largest tower of Warklesby's School of Magic, hardly a sound emitted from the galleries, set up specially to accommodate the large public interest in the case. Nobody dared to make a noise, lest they miss something, for the arrival of the jury was due any minute now.

Perhaps it was his age that made him so susceptible to the unbearable heat, Immanuel Robinson thought. He could not remember ever having been so uncomfortable on the judge's bench before. Perhaps, however, it had been the peculiar details of the case that had such an effect upon him. He had seen many a crime during his long career, though none came close to matching the extent and the sheer *evil* – there was no other word for it – of Vincent Wycliffe's deeds.

He didn't know whether the gaunt, stony stares of the victims' relatives or the heart-wrenching account of one of the few survivor's had been worse. He only knew that he had had to take two showers in quick succession that very evening.

He had been able to uphold the veneer of his impartiality during the trial, it was quite true. Yet never before had it appeared so hollow to him. The loss of objectivity frightened him. Retirement, he thought, had never been more appealing.

Strangely, the accused had seemed perfectly unperturbed by any of it. In all the many years in the magical courts of

1

England, Immanuel Robinson had never witnessed anything quite like it. He was no psychologist, of course, but he had seen his fair share of what experts deemed to be 'psychopathic sorcerers', menaces to their fellow witches and warlocks. And yet, there was something uniquely distant and merciless about the way Wycliffe sat there, neither ashamed nor frightened. At times, he thought he caught a glimpse of secret pleasure in those dark eyes as the details of his crimes came to the fore. And it made the judge's blood boil.

At last, the court usher announced the return of the jury with their final verdict. A moment later, the members of the jury – all wearing a sombre expression – filed through the door next to the uppermost gallery and made their way down the spiral staircase that led them directly to the jury box.

Judge Robinson scanned the many tense faces around him. The time of waiting had become unbearable for many in the galleries. People shouted 'murderer' and 'hang him', while others shook their fists at Wycliffe. Security warlocks were having trouble keeping angry spectators in line.

"Order," Judge Robinson boomed, his voice – magically enhanced – reverberating around the room.

Once more, he raised his handkerchief to his brow. As he did so, he couldn't help notice that his hand was shaking slightly. But when he spoke next, he was relieved to find that his voice was steady and authoritative.

"What is the verdict of the jury?"

"Your Lordship," the foreman of the jury said. "In the case of Wycliffe vs. the Magical Community of England, the jury has come to the following verdict…"

He opened the envelope in his hand, unfolding the single sheet of paper within.

"We find the accused guilty of all charges."

A roar of approval, accompanied by many more screams and cries demanding the hanging – or worse – of Wycliffe, permeated the chamber. This time, however, Judge Robinson did not call for order. He looked with the utmost disgust at Vincent Wycliffe, whose face had twisted into a sinister smirk. It was the only time in his career that he wished he had the power over life and death, as in the magical courts of old.

As the screams finally died down on their own, he addressed the court:

"Vincent Reginald Wycliffe, the jury has found you guilty of all charges. In light of the heinous and sadistic mode in which you perpetrated them, as well as the utter lack of sympathy for your victims, as showcased throughout the trial, I have no other choice but to sentence you to imprisonment for the rest of your natural life. Your powers will be stripped indefinitely. Your possessions are to be sold, and the proceeds to be distributed amongst the survivors and the relatives of your victims."

Slowly, Wycliffe rose his feet. Flanked by curtains of greasy blond hair, his grey eyes flashed dangerously at the judge.

"This is not the end," he spoke, his voice soft but clearly audible. "I shall return."

At Wycliffe's words, the courtroom erupted in turmoil. Hexes went flying everywhere, bouncing off the protective dome that Magical Law Enforcement officers had erected around the dock. Dozens of warlocks and witches were now scaling the balustrades, threatening to close in on Wycliffe.

Under fire from all sides, MLE officers dragged Wycliffe to an adjacent exit and pushed him through the door, where the judge knew that a prison transport was already waiting for him. The crowd swarmed the closed door, hammering on it with all their might, but they were too late. The trial of Wycliffe was finally over.

CHAPTER 2

"No, I cannot allow it," Barry said stubbornly, sitting on the dining room table and crossing his paws in front of him. "Utterly out of the question."

"But Barry," Val protested, "you'll love it once they've finished with it. And anyway, we'll be at the school, investigating the murders."

"No," Barry said flatly.

"It's got to be done at some point, you know," I said, looking up from my very tasty but slightly burnt bacon on the plate in front of me.

"I will not have clumsy workmen falling all over the place," Barry said, now beginning to pace up and down the table, his tail twitching in irritation. "Especially when I'm not there to make sure they don't get up to any mischief."

"Careful, Barry, your tail is in my coffee," I said, gently pushing it aside.

"Your library is falling apart, Barry!" Val said, with a mixture of affection and frustration. "And I'm sure they won't touch anything important. They won't even understand your research."

"Oh, you don't know these people," Barry said darkly. "All friendly and earthy one moment, next they'll be destroying – or worse, stealing – my research. No, I can't have it."

"Would you rather have another accident, Barry?" Val asked.

There was a short silence as Barry winced at the painful memories. One week ago, Barry had been working in his library deep into the night, as usual. Val and I had been roughly awakened by a terrifying shriek that carried right through the house. As Val sped over to Mrs. Faversham's cottage for help, I quickly guessed that the noise was coming from Barry's library. Though I thought at first it might have been some sort of experiment that had gone wrong, I was quickly corrected by the scene before me.

Barry had been lying at the bottom of a massive book shelf that reached right up to the ceiling. One of the contraptions – designed by my late great-aunt to provide Barry with access to all areas with relative ease – had lain broken and splintered next to him on the floor.

It had taken me the best part of two days to master the spells that would mend his bones again. It was an experience that neither of us wished to repeat. As one might imagine, Barry was not the easiest patient in the world.

Back in the present, however, Barry was desperately looking for a way to avoid repairs to his library.

"I'll just have to be more careful next time," he said. "I'm a cat, after all. I must have a few more lives left to play with."

"Sorry, Barry," I said. "But you're... well, you're getting on in years."

He drew himself up with what he considered to be a pose of dignified huffiness.

"Your point, Amanda?" he sniffed.

"Well, cats aren't supposed to be breaking bones when they fall. They're supposed to land on their feet."

"A minor oversight," he said. "I was lost in thought. Happens to great minds, you know. It's just part and parcel of my work."

"No, it isn't," Val said forcefully. "Because the library is getting repaired, isn't it, Amy?"

"I'm sorry, Barry, but it's my final word. We don't want you to get hurt again."

"Not physically, perhaps," he said morosely. "But the *emotional* pain of losing years of work might just be unbearable..."

"OK, here's the deal, Barry," I said. "I'll turn anyone who dares to steal your research into a frog. How about that?"

Barry pondered the unexpected offer for a while.

"A mouse might be more fitting, but I'm grateful for the sentiment nonetheless, Amanda," he said cheerfully. "But I want Mrs. Faversham to check in on them every day."

Val beamed at both of us.

"So, now we've got that out of the way, we should better start packing," Val said.

"Agreed," I said. "By the way, how are we getting to Warklesby's, anyway?"

"We arrive by magic, of course," said Barry.

He couldn't quite hide the relish in his voice at my complete ignorance.

"Right, so we fly there by broom, I take it?"

"No, it's too well hidden for that," he said loftily. "It's built into a rock in the mountains, you see. No, the school can only be accessed safely through a portal system. Luckily, your great-aunt had one connected to the house ages ago."

"A... a portal is in the house?" Val asked, slightly unnerved.

"Yes," Barry said. "But no need to fret. It cannot be activated unless permission is given. A little like a door to a house, if you will. You can approach and knock, but someone still has to let you in."

"I see. So where is this portal?" I asked. "I'm sure I've been in every room of the house by now. I haven't seen anything like that."

"It's behind the portrait in the living room. *My* portrait, in fact."

"Naturally," I said, rolling my eyes at Val, who started to giggle.

Barry, however, looked rather pleased with himself.

"I'd better head upstairs," said Val. "I still have some light packing to do."

"OK," I said. "I'll see you later."

***

After Mrs. Faversham had cleared away the remnants of our breakfasts, I went upstairs to finish off my own packing. Following the drastic events in Scotland earlier this year, I had come to appreciate Fickleton House even more than before. More than ever, its solid walls promised a security that the outside world definitely seemed to lack these days.

As I walked through the winding corridors with their familiar, dark wood panelling, I thought how significant it was that I had come to cherish Fickleton House so much. Before becoming a witch, I had always felt at home in the world, as well as being trusting of the people who surrounded me. Now, however, the memories from the lighthouse crept into my dreams whenever I wasn't expecting them. After all, who really knew how many other sorcerers roamed the country? Perhaps less than I currently imagined, though it certainly didn't feel that way.

And now, I'd be going into a school full of witches and warlocks. I was excited, yet afraid at the same time. Despite the fact that I worked hard to improve my magical abilities, I hadn't been a witch for long. I had never lived amongst spellcasters, excluding Barry, of course. His abilities, however, were greatly diminished as a cat. And though he often spoke of being close to a breakthrough in therianthropic retransformations and thus regaining his power, Val and I secretly agreed that it was wishful thinking rather than realistic hope that he'd ever be able to turn back into a warlock again. For the first time, therefore, I'd be surrounded by hundreds of expert spellcasters once I set foot in Warklesby's School of Magic. That fact alone, I was sure, would certainly make any detective work a lot more difficult.

Trying to push my worries aside, it took me the best part an hour to pack the rest of my things. Before we could depart, I still had to phone the workmen, who'd be doing up Barry's library. I had already contacted a local man on Mrs. Faversham's recommendation, but I still had to give the signal that we could go ahead as planned.

I briskly crossed the large, open grounds of Fickleton House that led to Mrs. Faversham's cosy little cottage. Since magic was used so much in the main house, electrical equipment didn't work there. At first, I had been irritated at having to use Mrs. Faversham's telephone every time I wanted to call someone, though I had come to appreciate that I was no longer at the beck and call of modernity around the clock.

Mrs. Faversham had left a note on her door, informing me that she was out shopping and would be back shortly. Fortunately, she had left the door open.

I stepped inside, carefully cleaning my shoes on the mat, and made for the sitting room where the telephone was located.

And then, I heard an oddly muffled voice from within. I froze, listening intently. It was definitely not Mrs. Faversham. Had someone broken into her cottage while she was out?

I fumbled for my wand in my pocket, but it wasn't there. Foolishly, I must have left it with the rest of my things in my room. With nothing else to hand, I grabbed the sturdiest-looking umbrella under the hat stand and crept slowly towards the door.

It was ajar, so I pushed it open very gently, ready to strike at the slightest movement. But the sight that met my eyes was very different than I had expected.

On the small table near the window, Barry was crouched in front of the telephone, a handkerchief covering his mouth.

"Yes, that's right," Barry was saying. "There was a

mistake... Yes... I want you to cancel all arrangements you made with Miss Sheridan... That's right... On whose authority, you say? Why the Earl of Barrington's, of course! ... Never heard of him? Now listen here, you little ..."

"Barry!" I exclaimed, caught been laughter and indignation. "What on earth are you doing?"

Caught red-handed, Barry gazed up at me in shock. After a moment, he cursed loudly and then placed a paw on the hook to hang up the call. With the other, he removed the handkerchief from the speaker.

"Well," he said drily, "it was worth a try."

"Barry," I said sternly, "you're just being silly. That library of yours is a death trap. And it ends here."

"It didn't work anyway," he said, waving a paw irritably. "The firm wouldn't change the booking. Social rank, it appears, counts for less and less these days."

"So does common sense," I said, supressing a grin at Barry's antics.

I picked up the receiver and redialled. The man at the other end had a very strange tale to tell indeed, one that involved an imaginary earl who had called them to cancel the order.

"Oh, yes," I said, "that was my... my grandfather. He's a little disoriented at times."

Ignoring Barry's furious visual signs of protestation, I confirmed for them to start the very next day. Mrs. Faversham was to let them in and out of the house. Barry did not look pleased, but, for his own good, I remained adamant.

***

A quarter of an hour later, I was back in my room in the main house again, with my bags all carefully stacked next to the door.

I had made only a few alterations since moving into

Fickleton House. Val had discovered a painting of my late great-aunt in the attic a few weeks ago, and I had decided to hang it up in my bedroom. There were no photographs around the house, so this was the only image I had of her. The painting depicted a woman in her late forties, with dark, curly hair, already interspersed with specks of grey. She looked impressive, though there was also a nurturing kindness that I thought the artist had captured very well in her smile and the crinkles around her eyes.

Though I had never known her, of course, I felt I owed her a great deal. Placing her portrait on the wall was one way, however inadequate, of showing my gratitude. It was a great pity that I hadn't had the chance to get to know her, though I always enjoyed it whenever Barry talked about her.

Having packed all of my bags, I drew the curtains of my room. We didn't know how long we'd be gone, so cramming everything I might need into my two large suitcases was something of a conundrum in itself. In the end, I was forced to leave some of my things behind. Perhaps, I thought, with the portal in place, there was surely a way to retrieve some of them later, if needed.

Stepping out into the corridor, I was must about to make for the stairs when I heard a wheezing sound coming from the unlit corridor to my right. For one mad moment, I thought some sort of stray dog had miraculously found its way into Fickleton House. I dropped my suitcases, squinting my eyes to see what was going on in the darkness. It took me a moment to register who it was.

"Val!" I exclaimed, laughing. "What on earth are you doing?"

Val, puffing like a train, was teetering dangerously from side to side. She was balancing three suitcases of various sizes in each hand, a heavy-looking rucksack on her back, as well as what looked like a large, purple hat box that she was carrying by means of a string in her mouth.

She stopped in order to answer me, but that was a grave

mistake. The hat box dropped to the floor. Trying to break stop it from falling with one desperate but futile dash forward, sending bags and boxes flying in the air and then towards the staircase.

"Amy, quick!" she yelled. "Do something!"

Pulling my wand as fast as I could, I directed my wand at the luggage.

"Levitate!"

The assortment of bags, boxes, and suitcases came to a halt in mid-air as though attached to invisible strings. Val inched forward slowly, as though scared she might cause them to fall again if she moved too quickly, and plucked them out of the air one by one.

"Val," I said, "is this your idea of *light packing*?"

"Oh, don't be silly, Amy," she said, laughing. "This isn't my stuff – it's Barry's."

"Barry's? But he's a cat, for crying out loud, what does he need all this for?" I said.

But before Val could answer, a dark, feline figure had appeared from the depths of the corridor.

"These," Barry said in a majestic tone, "are all the books I require to teach."

"You needn't have brought your entire library," I said.

"It is only a small, though absolutely crucial, part of it, I assure you," Barry said smartly. "And since I cannot prevent you from turning my quarters upside down, I decided to take the most valuable tomes with me."

"Easy for you to say, you didn't have to carry them," said Val.

"Why didn't you just ask me, Val? I could have whisked them downstairs by magic in a matter of minutes."

"Sorry, Amy," she said. "I couldn't find you. I guessed you were with Mrs. Faversham or something. Thought this'd be faster."

"Alright," I said. "We'd better get started. When… erm… is the portal due, Barry?"

"Portals aren't *due*, Amanda, they're…"

"Please, Barry, just tell me when we're leaving," I said, trying to avoid an unnecessary lecture.

"The next cycle," he said huffily, "is in about fifteen minutes."

"Good, let's catch that cycle, shall we?" I said.

"But I haven't even packed all my introductory works to elemental magic yet. Lord knows what these workmen will do with them if they get their hands on them."

With one last sharp look at Barry designed to quell any further resistance, I began magicking the luggage downstairs, followed by a relieved Val and a grumbling Barry.

Having arrived safely downstairs, the living room looked a lot smaller with all of our bags inside. On Barry's instructions, I performed a levitating charm on his portrait – pretending to lose control in the middle of the process, which had Val laughing heartily and Barry cursing at me.

"Let it go, Amy," said Val, wiping a tear from her cheek. "He'll have a heart attack if you don't."

"Not so *fast*, Amanda," Barry said angrily. "Really, if you think this is funny, I don't know what to say."

"It's just a little harmless teasing, Barry," said Val.

"Don't worry, it's safe with me," I said. "Now, it's off the wall. What do we do next?"

Evidently, Barry contemplated whether he should answer immediately or not. Finally, however, he must have come to the conclusion that the most dignified approach was to ignore the entire affair.

"We must reveal the portal," said Barry, pointing with his paw to the bare patch on the wall where the painting had been a moment earlier.

"And how do we do that?"

"Draw your wand along a line away from the fireplace, at the bottom. Here, you see. Draw it in a straight line, the portal is a lot larger than the portrait, mind. Now, when you're ready, keep repeating the following words: Porta aperire."

"Porta aperire," I said, murmuring it all the while I was edging my wand along the borders of the invisible portal.

Immediately, a line of bright green began to emerge, thin yet pronounced. To fully redraw the other three lines of the portal, I had to climb onto a nearby chair, as physical contact between the wand and the wall were mandatory.

At last, I had joined up the last line, and stepped down from the chair. The green light seemed to be pulsating now, like a geometric heart. The pulses were accompanied by a rushing sound that faded in and out.

"And now?" asked Val.

"We knock," said Barry.

I considered this to be part of the house metaphor Barry had used earlier.

"And how do we knock in the magic world?" I asked.

"For once," Barry said, smirking, "it is the same as in the heb world. Just knock three times, but make sure it's in the middle of the square, otherwise they won't hear it clearly."

I stepped forward, feeling rather foolish, and tapped the bare wall with my knuckles. Once, twice, three times. The green lines continued to vibrate around the spot, but nothing happened.

"I don't think it's working, Barry," said Val.

"Wait," he said confidently. "They will answer eventually. It's a busy school, after all."

And sure enough, after a minute – or perhaps it was longer – the lines stopped pulsating but instead shone a bright white that blinded all of us for a moment. In the middle of the portal, a sign appeared. Though I was sure it was impossible, it seemed familiar somehow. It was a black hedgehog on a blue background.

"That," Barry said, reading our bewildered expressions correctly, "is the school emblem."

"A hedgehog?" asked Val in disbelief.

"It is a most noble animal," said Barry. "But don't worry, they will bore the pants off of you at the school in regard to all of this trivia. Quickly, now, before the portal closes again. We have to get our luggage in first."

I grabbed the suitcase that was closest to me. Stepping in front of the portal, I gently placed it against the wall – or so I thought. For the wall was no longer solid, and the suitcase went right through, vanishing in an instant as if being sucked in by a miniature black hole. Val, desperate not to miss the fun, tried one of her bags, with the same effect. Soon enough, we had all but a few handbags inside the portal.

First, it was Barry's turn to go through, and then Val. I had to step through last because I had to speak the incantation that would close the portal from our side. It was a delayed-action spell of Barry's own invention that no longer necessitated a witch or warlock to remain behind at the point of entry.

After Barry and Val had passed through the portal, it was my turn. But I found myself hesitant to follow them. For one mad moment, I thought of calling the whole thing off. Something within me wanted to stay in Fickleton House, protected by its ancient walls, with little else to worry about than Mrs. Faversham burning my bacon every once in a while.

But then, as I remembered the desperate letter we had received from Warklesby's School of Magic only a short while ago, the madness passed as soon as it had come. A mystery was waiting to be solved, and I was not one to shirk from such a task. With three waves of my wand, I spoke the final incantation that would seal the portal. Then, looking one last time at the house that had become such a comfort to me, I walked in front of the blazing portal. I tested it with my right foot first, immediately feeling it suck me in, though not unpleasantly so. Pressing my lips together in determination, I stepped through, leaving

Fickleton House behind me.

CHAPTER 3

Transport within the portal system was a lot more violent and uncomfortable than I had anticipated. It was like being sucked into a massive vacuum cleaner. As blackness engulfed me, I felt my arms and legs being pulled in every conceivable direction. My head was jerked to and fro, as though I was a ball in an old arcade machine.

Then, with a dull smack, I landed head first on a dirty carpet, inhaling a mouthful of dust in the process. Coughing furiously, it took me a while to bring my new surroundings into focus.

Barry and Val, both wearing bemused looks on their faces, were already waiting for me. They weren't the only people present, however. There seemed to be a welcome party specially for us, but I could see, probably due to my less than elegant appearance, that they were not impressed by what they saw.

Still feeling my bones and limbs ache from the portal experience, I gingerly got to my feet. The room we were in resembled a waiting area in a doctor's office as I imagined it must have been around the early 1900s. The furniture was antique and worn-out. On the walls, paintings depicted witches and warlocks, all dressed in robes and pointy hats from various periods of wizarding history. There was no sign of our luggage, however.

Barry smoothly stepped forward to make the introductions.

"Headmistress, deputy headmaster, this is Amanda Sheridan."

There was a slight, awkward pause.

"And this," Barry continued, "is the headmistress of Warklesby's School of Magic, Muriel Hall."

Muriel Hall was a thin woman in her late forties. She had brown hair, reaching well below her shoulders. Though it was still full, regular strands of grey permeated it. The deep crinkles on her forehead, as well as the bags beneath her eyes, gave the impression of someone young who had aged rapidly within a very short amount of time. But although her looks were fading, I could tell that she must have once been an attractive woman.

"How do you do?" she said, with a rather vacant smile as she shook my hand. "I hope your journey was pleasant enough."

"Well," I said, trying to loosen up the atmosphere a little bit, "I need a few more times to get used to portal travel."

The tall man standing next to the headmistress snorted, a look of superiority on his face.

"This, Amanda," Barry said, "is the deputy headmaster, Clement Harper."

The dislike was instant, as well as mutual. Harper couldn't have been much older than thirty-five, though he had made every effort in his appearance to look the part of a more experienced and seasoned man. His dress robes were meticulous though boring, as was his sleek blond hair that he had combed backward. He wore round black glasses that gave him the air of an ill-tempered bureaucrat.

We shook hands for the briefest of moments, eyeing one another in silence.

The headmistress seemed oblivious to this, however. She smiled again, beckoning all of us to follow her.

"We will have more privacy in my office," she said.

With one last expression of disdain, the deputy headmaster turned on his heel and followed her. Val looked at me with raised eyebrows. Clearly, someone wasn't too keen on having us here.

"Excellent start," I breathed to Val. "Always great to have a warm welcome."

"Yeah," said Val. "I wonder what the rest of the staff

are like."

"I think it can only really go uphill from here," I said softly.

We passed along several corridors with stone walls. They looked much older than the room we had arrived in, though they were also in much better condition. Students bustled past us, chatting to one another as they headed for their next class. Life, apparently, was continuing as normal, though there was a nervous, restless energy about it.

At last, the headmistress and her deputy came to a halt in front of a small archway. Beyond it, a narrow stone spiral staircase led upward.

"Only fifteen floors to go," the headmistress said heavily, as though she were speaking more to herself than to us.

Our little party traipsed up the stairs, which were extremely narrow and steep, so that I had to help Val on multiple occasions. Panting furiously atop the fifteenth and final staircase, a broad landing – adorned with a carpet of gold and red – led us straight to a pair of ornate doors made of oak. With a wave of her wand, Headmistress Hall opened them for us.

We stepped into what might have been the most beautiful office I had ever seen in my life. The rough stone slabs that had dominated the corridors and staircases so far had been replaced by marble. A massive desk made of a dark wood – mahogany perhaps – spanned almost the entire width of the room at the far end. Behind it, large windows overlooked fields of green and yellow as far as the eye could see, stretching down into a woodland valley.

Sitting down in a leather armchair behind her desk, the headmistress beckoned us to sit on the three chairs opposite her. Val, Barry, and I each took a seat. Harper, in any case, seemed to prefer to stand. With a tired flick of her wand, Muriel Hall whipped up tea and biscuits for all of us.

"First, I'd like to welcome you to Warklesby's School of

Magic," she began slowly. "It really is a wonderful institution... or *was*, rather, before all this... awful business began."

"I'm sorry to hear it," I said sincerely.

Deputy Headmaster Harper scowled and looked out of the window. As before, the headmistress seemed to take no notice of his disapproval.

"Thank you for saying so, Miss Sheridan," she continued. "It really was a shock to everyone here."

"So what happened exactly?" I asked. "The letter only spoke of several kidnappings at the school but didn't provide any further details."

"... a *series* of kidnappings," corrected Harper irritably. "It'd be a miracle if the same person *wasn't* responsible for all three of them."

"Yes, indeed," said Headmistress Hall, nodding her head. "That is what it looks like. But you never know. Magical Law Enforcement certainly believe it to be the same person, but they have been unable to find the perpetrator. And I'm afraid to say that, I..."

She paused, looking at her desk for a moment, evidently trying to fight back the tears that were on their way.

"I believe what the headmistress is trying to say," Harper said, pompously shifting his glasses, "is that if we don't find out who is committing these crimes, the school will have to be closed."

"But that would also mean you wouldn't be able to track down the guilty party anymore," I said. "Is that right?"

The headmistress nodded heavily.

"That is, in fact, why we have asked you to come here, Miss Sheridan. With the Earl of Barrington acting as our substitute professor for water magic, you will have an advantage that the police do not. You will be able to blend in with the staff and students."

"Headmistress," Harper blurted out, unable to contain himself any longer, "if I may. The situation calls for trained professionals, not amateurs."

"Hey," said Val, narrowing her eyes, "who are you calling amateurs?"

"With all due respect, headmistress," Harper continued, though his manner suggested quite the contrary, "our *guests* have no formal education in detective work. The cat is even incapable of wielding a wand properly, while Miss Sheridan would require decades of training before she could even confront one of our pupils, let alone a dangerous sorcerer."

This time, it was Barry's and my turn to protest. Struggling to resist my urge to slap him across the face immediately, I stood up, shaking slightly.

"Excuse me?" I said angrily.

"I resent your tone of voice," said Barry, who was also on all fours.

"Well, then why don't you…" Harper began, turning on Barry.

But the headmistress lifted her hand to stop him. It was a surprisingly authoritative gesture that must have caught all of us by surprise, for we all stopped arguing at once. Headmistress Hall looked sternly at her deputy headmaster.

"Clement, we have been over this several times before. And my decision in this matter is final, as I have told you also. Our guests stay. And you will do everything you can to aid them in their attempt to catch this murderer. Have I made myself clear?"

Harper, realising he had pushed it too far, stared at us and then the headmistress, his mouth opening and closing again like a fish, though no sound came out of it. Slowly – though resentment was etched across his entire face – he nodded.

"Yes, headmistress. Forgive me," he said coldly, rearranging his round glasses.

"What matters the most," said the headmistress, returning to her tired and weary way of speaking again, "is that we all want this sorcerer caught. The priority is to the safety of this school and to its pupils. The *Spellcasting Parents' Association* quite rightly demanded the immediate resolution of this matter. They are worried about their children, and so should we."

Privately, I thought that Harper certainly didn't look as though he had the same priorities. His lips were white with repressed rage, though he remained perfectly still as he stared out into the fields.

"I have taken," the headmistress continued, "every possible precaution. No student is to walk the corridors alone. Teachers are to report any missing pupils immediately. At night, every dormitory reports to me directly if anyone is out of bed. But, until this sorcerer is caught, we can do little else."

"So what do we know about the case?" I asked.

"Well," the headmistress began, "it's a rather long story. I suppose I should start with… Vincent Wycliffe. Some thirty years ago, Wycliffe was here at the school as a student. He had been moderately gifted, not much better or worse than many of his peers. He specialised in earth magic. It was quite surprising, therefore, that after finishing school Wycliffe was promoted to the post of assistant teacher by the then head of department for earth magic, Professor MacKenzie."

Headmistress Hall shifted rather uncomfortably in her chair.

"I knew both of them, because I was a young pupil here at the time, too. Wycliffe was several years older than I was. There had been a lot of talk about his promotion, even amongst the students, for there had been far more talented candidates available. But nobody really thought about it much after a while. Wycliffe, though not brilliant, did his work, and so that seemed to be the end of the matter. Biscuits, anyone?"

"Erm, no thanks," I said, confused at the headmistress's sudden break in her story. "So what happened next?"

"Well," she said, absent-mindedly reaching for one of the biscuits herself, "nothing happened – or at least, nobody was aware of what was developing in that mind of his – brewing, you might say. But then, years later, when I was in my last year of school, mysterious things began to occur at the school. You see, I had my own academic hopes for the future, and so I worked as a student helper in several departments. You know, menial tasks such as copying or preparing notes. One such job was in earth magic, and so I saw Professor MacKenzie and Vincent Wycliffe quite regularly. Their relationship, so much was obvious to me at the time, was bad – and it was deteriorating further."

"You mean, they quarrelled openly?" asked Barry.

"Yes," she said, a vague expression on her face. "Yes, you see, Wycliffe demanded more time for his research, wishing to reduce his teaching duties. Professor MacKenzie, however, refused. In fact, he even increased Wycliffe's teaching hours."

"Why would he do that?" I asked. "Just to spite him?"

"Perhaps," she said. "There's certainly no shortage of ill-feeling in the academic world, I can assure you. And, as I said, they didn't get on very well anymore. However, I think there was another reason. A less personal one. This is hindsight, of course – judging from what Wycliffe did later on – but I can only assume that MacKenzie had found out in which direction Wycliffe's research was going."

"A very sinister direction, I might add," the deputy headmaster said suddenly.

"What sort of research was he involved in?" I asked the headmistress.

"Necromancy," the deputy headmaster interjected before she could answer herself.

Val looked rather bewildered.

"It is a forbidden branch of earth magic," Barry added helpfully. "It hasn't been practised legally in centuries."

"You mean, Wycliffe was trying to resurrect the dead?" I asked, horrified.

"In essence, yes," the headmistress said. "We believe that he destroyed the majority of his work before he was captured, so it is difficult to tell how deep he was into necromancy at the time."

"So what happened next?" I asked.

The headmistress didn't answer immediately, but gazed out of the windows behind her for a while. Her expression was impossible to read. Yet it seemed to me to be more vacant and adrift than ever. Was this her peculiar way of remembering the events surrounding Wycliffe's crimes? Somehow, I had the impression that there was something more, something deeper, that seemed to be eating away at her.

"I think," she said quietly, "it started with little things. As it did a few weeks ago, again."

"What do you mean?" I asked, shifting to the edge of my chair so that I could better understand what she was saying.

"You must understand," she continued, turning around to face us again, "that I only gained full access to this information after I had become headmistress. The headmaster had kept these things secret at the time. They aren't open to the public. But I recognised the patterns quickly enough."

"What pattern was that?" I asked.

It felt as if I were trying to draw blood from a stone, as she paused yet again, staring at us, unable to continue. The deputy headmaster, no doubt feeling impatient, spoke next.

"What the headmistress is trying to say is that..."

"Please, Clement," she said in a tired voice, closing her eyes, "let me explain fully to our guests. They need to know *everything*, do you understand?"

It was quite evident that he strongly disagreed, but he pressed his lips so tightly together until they went white in his effort to stop himself from speaking. The headmistress drew back and opened a drawer at the bottom of her desk. She retrieved a piece of paper. The writing was tiny, but it looked like some sort of list to me.

"You must understand that, as necromancy is prohibited by magical law, there are naturally very few scholars who have delved deeply enough into the subject to understand it. It is forbidden knowledge, and it is thus quite common for theoretical researchers or historians to become suspect. That makes it rare, because few would choose to meddle with it with such a heavy cost attached to it. But, as you might also imagine, there are some who seek it for the sake of the forbidden. A juvenile impulse, often, to test the boundaries of our world."

She sighed, as though a great burden was beginning to lift.

"From my very first year onward, there had been rumours of necromancy amongst the students – and even amongst the staff. Most people didn't take these allegations seriously. The official school line, as expressed by many staff members and the headmaster himself, was that these stories were suitable only for frightening the gullible and the young, and that they lacked any basis in actual fact."

She fidgeted slightly, playing around the corners of the list in front of her.

"At the time, we didn't know that they were lying to us. As the magical community found out much later, the evidence was there. Many had tried to convince the headmaster that something evil was brewing within his school, though he chose to ignore it until it was far too late. He simply couldn't believe that anyone at the school would do such things. And so, he took the easy approach and denounced all those who warned him as conspiracy theorists and troublemakers.

"Yet, the signs were there. Soon enough, markings appeared in the corridors of the school. They depicted the forbidden symbols of necromancy, the staff and skull, as well as the bone and the book. These acts in and of themselves, of course, would have simply been viewed as forms of teenage vandalism and provocation. But other, more sinister occurrences soon weighed heavily upon the school. There were reports by students that they had seen secret rituals in the woods nearby, well beyond the gaze of authority. A member of staff reported a similar event close to the school's graveyard, where many accomplished scholars and teachers have been put to rest.

"To make things worse, a series of mysterious break-ins plagued the school at the time. Specific roots, plants, and rare powders were stolen. Few – if anyone – recognised the importance of the specific magical ingredients that went missing, of course. The headmaster, still wilfully ignorant, insisted that these were no different from other acts of theft in the past."

Headmistress Hall paused, breathing heavily again as she suddenly looked at her office door. For a moment, I thought she was afraid of someone eavesdropping.

"Of course," she continued, though in a somewhat lower voice, "they were nothing of the sort. Taken as a whole, these precise ingredients had been used for millennia in the abhorrent practice of necromancy, though the problem at the time was, as I said, that it took an expert to recognise this.

"Soon enough, people began to vanish. Though the crimes were investigated, the working assumption was that the students in question had in fact simply run away from school. But as more and more students disappeared, even the headmaster had to admit that something was seriously wrong. The MLE was contacted, and an investigation began, though with few results. The problem was that nobody had drawn the connection with the markings and the stolen ingredients.

"Luckily, a historian of magic who had specialised in the

history of necromancy, one of the very few academics who did at the time, had come to Warklesby's as a guest lecturer a few weeks earlier. He immediately recognised the pattern when the issue of stolen ingredients from the school's supplies was raised during a staff meeting. He asked for a complete list of missing items and soon confirmed that, due to the amounts and ratios stolen, they were most certainly intended for the dark practice of necromancy. The rest, I'm afraid, is history."

She looked at us as though the matter were settled, but Val appeared to be just as puzzled as I was. I was just about to inquire about the rest of the story when there was a loud knock on the door.

"Come," said the headmistress.

An adolescent youth entered the room. He was wearing a student's uniform, though he had taken off his warlock's hat, revealing untidy black hair. The headmistress squinted slightly so that she could recognise the face. Then, she clucked her tongue in disapproval.

"Again, Ross?" she said, a twinkle in her eye. "What was it this time?"

"Inappropriate answers in class, ma'am."

"How many more detentions are you determined to acquire this term?" she asked.

"I've always been one for records, headmistress," Ross said cheekily. "Beg your pardon, ma'am."

He smiled in mock-apology. To my surprise, the headmistress seemed to be secretly enjoying the encounter, and she was trying her best to suppress a smile in front of her deputy. Harper, however, was less than amused. He cleared his throat violently.

"Expulsion from the school is also a record of sorts, Ross," he fumed. "Remember that."

"Indeed," the headmistress said, though I could see by her twitching mouth that she didn't seriously consider it. "I will deal with you later. Justice will have to wait a little longer, even for you, Julian Ross."

The youth made a ridiculously low bow, flashing his grin at all of us again as his handsome head emerged again, and was just about to turn around when the headmistress stopped him.

"Wait," she said, her tone suddenly much sharper than before. "How long have you been outside the door, Ross?"

"Me?" he said innocently, blinking. "Why, only a few minutes, headmistress."

"Did you hear anything you shouldn't have?" the deputy headmaster, his arms crossed, barked at him.

"Of course not, sir. I would never…"

"Spare us the act, Ross," the deputy spat. "Out with it. What did you hear?"

Ross, sensing real consequences for a change, switched gears quickly. His mocking features rearranged themselves into a remarkably good impression of someone who had been wrongfully accused of an awful crime.

"Headmistress, I *did* hear voices inside, so I decided to wait. But I didn't hear anything specific. Then, I thought I'd knock all the same, since I didn't know how long your meeting would be. I didn't hear a thing. I swear it. That's the honest truth."

The headmistress eyed him with a mixture of indulgence and suspicion. Finally, she turned to the deputy headmaster, giving him the briefest of nods.

"Deputy Headmaster Harper will oversee that you are *fairly* punished, Ross."

"But, headmistress, I…" he spluttered.

"That will do, Ross," she said. "I assure you that you will not be expelled, but I cannot attend to it myself right now… under the present circumstances. Clement, would you mind escorting Ross downstairs?"

"With pleasure, headmistress," Harper said menacingly.

Julian Ross had no choice but to follow the deputy headmaster downstairs. But I could tell that his curiosity was sparked. What was so important that the headmistress wanted to conceal it from him?

After they had left, the headmistress waited for a while longer. She got up, periodically looking at the closed door, pacing around the room until she was satisfied that Harper and Ross were definitely out of earshot.

"Julian Ross is a bit of a rascal," she said, smiling, "but he has his heart in the right place. However, we cannot be too careful these days. I would advise you, also, to trust no one."

"I will certainly make no exception for your deputy, madam," said Barry, still offended at Harper's earlier impertinence.

She frowned.

"I understand your feelings, but you mustn't be too hard on Clement. He wants this situation resolved as much as anyone else. Even though he would go about it in a different way. Now, where were we?"

"I think you were going to tell us about how Wycliffe was captured," I said.

I felt a bit foolish for asking since it seemed that everyone in the magical world knew who he was and what he had done. Nevertheless, I needed the facts.

"Oh, yes. Well, after it had been established that necromancy was involved – and had been ignored for so long – there was nothing less than a political earthquake. The headmaster was dismissed and shunned. Forced into retirement, he died a few years later – I think more of shame than anything else, if such a thing is possible.

"Meanwhile, the MLE had taken control of the school. They combed the entire castle from dungeon to spire in an effort to find the perpetrator. At first, they found nothing. But then, the professor for earth magic went missing."

"You mean, Professor MacKenzie, Wycliffe's boss?" Val asked.

"Yes," she said. "Suspicion fell immediately on the

entire department. Once more, they searched the private rooms of all teachers, student helpers, and research scholars connected to the department of earth magic."

"So, they had searched them before?" I asked.

"Indeed, Miss Sheridan," she said. "It was a decision informed by prejudice. The department of earth magic was the very first to fall under scrutiny…"

"… because necromancy is a branch of earth magic," I said.

"Correct," she said, nodding. "I myself was never quite convinced of the necessity of that connection. You see, although it *is* true that it is considered to be a part of earth magic, many of the principles of necromancy, aside from the moral dimension of course, are so very different from – let us say – 'usual' earth magic. Warlocks or witches specialised in earth magic, therefore, would hardly have any advantage in terms of actual ability or knowledge."

"But Wycliffe *was* a specialist in earth magic," said Barry, frowning.

"Yes, it is quite true. I'm merely pointing it out so that you might consider all options in your own investigations."

"I see," he said.

"So, during the search, they found some incriminating evidence in Wycliffe's room the second time around, then?" I asked.

"That's right," she said. "The peculiar thing was that he had survived the first search unscathed. Perhaps he thought that the danger had passed. Or maybe he was forced to move some of his research from his other hiding places. In any case, the MLE arrested him immediately, but unfortunately he was able to burn a lot of his work as they closed in, so that the true extent of his crimes remains unknown. The fire he set almost consumed the entire East Tower."

"Did Wycliffe confess?" asked Val.

"Yes, he did," the headmistress said. "Though for some

reason he wouldn't disclose where he had dumped the bodies. Perhaps he had hopes of continuing his work at a later date in case he escaped. He spoke of his 'return' many times during the trial. Some of his victims were found later, deep within the woods. Others, well, they're technically still missing, though nobody has any doubts about their fate."

"Did he succeed in…" Val began, though unable to finish the horrible thought.

"I believe that the official judgment," Headmistress Hall said, hesitating slightly, "was that Wycliffe had tried but failed in his attempts at necromancy."

"But you thought otherwise," I said.

She stared at me for a while, measuring her words.

"Yes," she said, her bags under eyes as pronounced as ever, "I do, Miss Sheridan, though I have no proof. You see, the authorities were desperate to calm the situation, as far as that was possible. Once the full horror of Wycliffe's crimes became known – thirteen victims to date, though possibly even more – people felt that the those in charge had failed them. Most witches and warlocks agreed. Myself included. Others – though a minority no doubt – felt otherwise. It was surprising how many people admired Wycliffe."

"A monster like him?" Val asked incredulously.

"I know," the headmistress said. "It is hard to believe now. But at the time, some felt that Wycliffe had pushed the boundaries of magic further than anyone else. There were anonymous letters to the press, demanding his release and legalisation of necromancy. They were ignored, of course, so Wycliffe's followers burnt down the Magical Courthouse in London where the trial was supposed to take place. So the trial was moved here, to the school, in the large West Tower. It had been closed for the summer entirely, and its isolated and undisclosed location was ideal for the trial, though they still allowed spectators to attend."

"So Wycliffe was found guilty?" I asked.

"Oh, yes," the headmistress said. "The evidence was incontrovertible. He repeated his confession, in fact. Apparently, Professor MacKenzie had finally been willing to act on his suspicions regarding his assistant and had intended to turn him in. Throughout the trial, Wycliffe showed no remorse whatsoever. He even goaded some of the victims' families. It was horrible. Many demanded the reinstitution of the death penalty, but of course, the law was the law. He was stripped of his powers and sentenced to solitary confinement for life, the harshest punishment in our world. In a manner of speaking, those who deemed it too light a sentence got their way in the end, though."

"What do you mean?" I asked.

"Wycliffe was murdered in prison, about a year ago. A petty squabble amongst prisoners in the yard. He was buried in a secret location, for the general mood was still tense – even after all those years. And that should have been the end of it."

She stared at the door again, an almost paranoid look on her face. Perhaps it was the setting sun behind her, but the lines on her face seemed deeper and darker than before.

"But it wasn't the end. Now, twenty years after Wycliffe's crimes, it's starting again," she said in nothing more than a whisper. "The signs on the walls, the talk of necromancy. And disappearances, too. It's exactly how it was when he was at large the last time."

"You don't mean…" I began.

"There have been horrible rumours. Rumours that he has returned from the dead, seeking revenge. You've got to help us."

CHAPTER 4

She looked desperately at Val, Barry, and me. Somehow, it made the burden a lot heavier. It had felt a lot easier accepting the request in the form of a letter a few weeks ago. Now, however, the severity of the situation became a lot more pronounced.

"Of course, headmistress," I said. "We're here to provide any help we can."

"I'm counting on it," she said. "Your track record is indeed impressive. And some fresh pairs of eyes are what we really need in this dire situation."

She took the list that had been lying in front of her on the desk and handed it to me.

"This is a list I've compiled – on a strictly confidential level, you understand – of all the known locations of necromancer signs that were spotted throughout the school. Most of them have been erased, of course, for fear of frightening the students even further, if that's at all possible, that is. You will find the names of the missing people below. Two students and one teacher. In regard to the stolen supplies, you should better talk to our quarterwarlock, Henry Armbruster."

"Thank you, this will help a lot," I said, scanning the list. "Did the MLE find any leads?"

Headmistress Hall shook her head miserably.

"None at all," she said. "The entire school was searched multiple times. No office, dormitory, or staff room was spared. Not even mine. But they couldn't track down the missing people."

"And you think they're dead?" I asked.

"Yes," she said miserably. "It's the same pattern as… as last time when Wycliffe was active."

"Can you tell us more about the people who've gone missing?" I said. "Were there any specific circumstances we should know about?"

"Neither I nor the MLE could find any link between them. Peter Hucklebee was our professor for water magic – hence the need for a replacement," she said, inclining her head towards Barry. "He made no comment before he vanished. All of his things were left untouched. As for the two students, Robert Chesterton and Annabelle Swinton, were in their fifth and sixth years here, respectively. As far as we know, they had never even spoken to one another. We could find no connection between them in any dimension of their lives."

"So, you think it's a random selection of victims?" I asked.

"Well," she said, hesitantly, "I cannot know for certain, of course. But the evidence so far certainly indicates that there is no particular reason why they were taken."

"Does the MLE share your view?" asked Barry shrewdly. "That Wycliffe has somehow returned from the dead, I mean."

"I-I don't know," she said. "I'm not even sure myself. It seems impossible and yet... All I'm saying is that the pattern is exactly the same as last time. Some of the agents are old enough to remember what it was like all those years ago. But without bodies, or evidence that foul play is involved at all, there is very little they can do apart from searching the school. But the answer, I'm sure of it, must be somewhere in there."

She pointed at the list in my hand.

"Some tiny detail that we've overlooked so far," she continued. "You have all the school resources at your disposal, just contact me or Clement if you need anything."

"Thank you. Has anyone actually seen Wycliffe?" I asked.

"Not to my knowledge," said the headmistress slowly,

"but that doesn't mean it's not him. He could be in disguise."

"Posing as a student or a member of staff, you mean?" I asked.

"Precisely," said the headmistress.

"Is this possible to sustain for a long period of time?" I asked, turning to Barry.

"Oh, yes, certainly," said Barry. "A warlock trained in shapeshifting will have no problem doing that, since the transformations are minor in comparison to, say, turning into an animal. That wouldn't be the problem."

Barry hesitated.

"What's the matter?" Val asked.

"Well," he said, "I'm no expert in necromancy, but I've never heard of anyone reviving themselves."

"Maybe he had an accomplice," said Val.

"Or," I said, "it could be someone else. A copycat killer, mimicking Wycliffe's style?"

"Yes," Barry said, "that is also possible."

"Does anyone else know why we are here?" I asked, turning back to the headmistress.

"The school board does, but few members actually reside here at the castle. In fact, that only includes Professor Olsen at present."

"I see," I said. "We want to keep our cover for as long as possible."

"Of course," she said. "I have demanded the utmost secrecy of all of them, but I'll have another word with Professor Olsen. I'm sure he will understand."

I pocketed the list. Val and I got to our feet, and Barry hopped down from his chair. We shook hands (and paws) with the headmistress once more and headed for the beautiful oak doors that led out of her office.

***

Having descended the many stone steps again, I felt at a complete loss. Although I wouldn't have admitted it openly, I felt more like an amateur now than ever before. In our previous two cases, we had always slipped into them by accident. At Warklesby's School of Magic, however, things were different. We had been hired with the specific purpose of solving a mystery that even Magical Law Enforcement, with all their manpower and resources, couldn't crack. What, then, could be expected of us? Would most people presuppose our failure from the start? The deputy headmaster, I noted with a shudder of utter dislike, certainly believed that. But the thought of him telling the headmistress that he had been right all along was unbearable.

"Are you OK, Amy?" Val asked.

I swung around. She had that look on her face that told me she had been reading me like a book.

"I... sure, everything's fine," I lied.

"No, it's not," she said. "You can't fool an empathetic psychic, you know."

"I suppose I can't," I said, cheering up a little. "Especially when she's my best friend, too. So, where should we start?"

"The Great Hall, of course," said Barry confidently.

"Why there?" I asked.

"Because I'm hungry," he said.

We all laughed. Good old Barry, I thought, he always brought one back to the basics – and far away from the debilitating self-doubt that had crept into my thoughts.

"Well, at least Barry has his priorities right," said Val. "Let's have a meal and get a good night's rest. It's probably best to start fresh in the morning."

"How do we get to the hall, though?" I asked.

"I know the way," said Barry.

We followed him through one ancient stone corridor to another. And yet, each seemed to have a life of its own. The portraits, reaching back centuries, were fascinating in themselves. Arches to tiny passageways hid behind tapestries of all shapes and sizes. Suits of armour were one thing, but the peculiar life-sized waxwork figures of great spellcasters that were strewn throughout the castle made the hairs at the back of my neck stand on end. They were excellent replicas, and so it was sometimes difficult to distinguish between them and groups of students we passed on our way. For the most part, however, we encountered few people on our way to the Great Hall.

"How come you know the way around this massive place, Barry?" asked Val.

"I've been invited several times before to give lectures on therianthropy. Many years ago, though. Before my unfortunate… miscalculation. Ah, here we are. I can already smell the outstanding tuna they make here."

Val and I opened a pair of heavy wooden doors. A loud buzz of conversation and chatter hit us as though we had been struck by a wave. We were facing the most massive hall I had ever seen in my life. The ceiling was so high that the place could have well served as a cathedral. Beautiful baroque artwork and carvings decorated every inch of it. Long banners hung from the walls, while larger-than-life statues and waxworks covered every corner in sight. In the centre, a sea of witches and warlocks sat at long benches and ornate tables made of white marble.

As far as the eye could see, foods from every continent were being devoured by students and staff alike. Above their heads, dozens of empty plates whizzed away while full plates precariously teetered through the air until landing with a plonk in front of a hungry witch or warlock. If ever there was a feast worth having – this was it.

"This is amazing," said Val, awestruck. "Can't wait for our turn. What do you say, Amy?"

"We certainly won't starve in here, that's for sure," I said. "Come on, let's find a table."

"I think," said Barry haughtily, "they're expecting me at the staff table. Researchers also sit there. You'd better join me, or otherwise they might smell a rat."

It turned out that the staff table was at the far end of the hall, on a slightly elevated platform. About two dozen people were already sitting there, though there were ample empty seats left. To my dismay, I saw that the deputy headmaster was already there, deep in conversation with a white-haired man. Harper had evidently finished disciplining the mischievous Ross.

As we approached the table, Harper spotted us. In an ostentatious display of hospitality, he rose from his seat and walked over to our side of the table.

"Dear colleagues," he said, sporting a smile that did not extend to his eyes at all, "may I introduce the newest additions to our staff. This is the Earl of Barrington, who will be filling in for Professor Hucklebee. He presently resides in feline form. And his companions are his research assistants, Miss Sheridan and Miss Morgan."

The staff members present muttered the polite greetings but quickly returned to their original conversations. Val and Barry made for the nearest seats. I was just about to follow when deputy headmaster Harper placed a hand on my arm that felt more like a claw.

"Finished investigating for the day already, have we?" he whispered.

"Not quite," I said coldly, pushing his arm away. "Still a few staff members to go, starting at the top."

He stared at me for a moment. Then, rearranging his round glasses in what he thought was a gesture of superior contempt, he turned around and walked back to his seat.

"What an arrogant p…" I murmured to Val as I sat down next to her.

"… person?" said Val, grinning. "Yeah. One for our list of suspects, d'you reckon?"

"Definitely," I said darkly, an image of myself arresting

him in front of the entire school leaping into my mind's eye.

"I certainly wouldn't put it past him," said Val. "I just don't understand why he doesn't want us here. I mean, it's not as if the MLE got anywhere on its own."

"Perhaps he's afraid of the truth," I said, just as Harper glanced over to our side of the table.

"Aren't we all?" said Val wisely.

"But we've got to remain as objective as possible, I suppose," I said, sighing.

I tried to shake off my personal feelings as best I could. Avenging personal slights would have to be a secondary concern as long as the school was in such danger. And after all, I thought, no murderer would be this stupid. Or would he?

"Pity it's never the obvious ones," said Val, as though she were reading my mind. "Life really would be a lot easier, wouldn't it?"

"Yeah," I said. "But you never know. It could be a clever bluff."

Barry, who had grown impatient next us, began clawing at my arm.

"Ouch," I exclaimed, "what's the matter, Barry?"

"I'm hungry."

"Oh, alright," I said. "Let's get our meals, then."

Ordering food was perhaps the most enjoyable thing I had done for quite a while in regard to magic. You simply had to place your wand on the menu and speak the name of the dish out loud. I helped Val and Barry order theirs first, then ordered my own.

Meanwhile, the deputy headmaster seemed to have finished his meal. He got up and, without another word, left the Great Hall in what seemed to be quite a hurry. Personally, I felt that the air was a lot lighter after he had gone.

Seeing the deputy headmaster leave the table, several of his colleagues decided to follow suit. Perhaps a bit of Muriel

Hall's paranoia had attached itself to me, but it was difficult not to see them all his potentially guilty. At the same time, I made an effort to be as inconspicuous as possible. The later the staff got wind of our plans, the better.

It was extraordinary to see how, only a few minutes after we had made our order, several dishes zoomed through the hall and landed right in front of us on the table. I had ordered Yorkshire puddings with roast beef and gravy. I don't know whether it was the particularly magical way it had been cooked, but I had never tasted anything quite like it. It was absolutely delicious.

In the meantime, Barry had got himself into a full-fledged discussion on magical theory with the elderly man with white hair, who had previously been in conversation with the deputy headmaster. If ever there was a walking caricature of a professor, I thought, this man was it. His tousled and uncombed hair seemed to sprouting from his head at random. His spectacles, foggy and thick, made his eyes appear unusually tiny.

"Certainly, I-I agree," he was saying, with an affected stutter that seemed to be so common amongst many academics. "But surely, Farthing's theorem of therianthropic immutability still counts for *something*. I simply find it impossible to conceive of any plausible solution that would be able to discount it."

Barry, puffing slightly from intellectual exertion, countered the point in a similarly verbose yet unintelligible answer that outlined his own view of shapeshifting theory.

"Oh, I wish he wouldn't go on like that," Val whispered, rolling her eyes.

"I don't know," I said thoughtfully. "He's playing his role perfectly."

"He's not playing a role, Amy, he's just being himself."

"Perhaps you're right," I said, grinning. "At any rate, a thorough debate gives us time to observe the field without arousing too much suspicion."

The discussion raged on as we ate our meals. Gradually, the combatants were shifting towards personal attacks to make their point.

"F-forgive me, Lord Barrington," the white-haired man with the thick glasses said, "but therianthropy has progressed a great deal since your... erm... *unfortunate accident*. Many new spells have been invented."

"Many," Barry snarled across the table, "invented by myself, I might add. *I* pioneered some of the most decisive breakthroughs in therianthropy in the 20th century!"

"A shame you cannot wield a wand to prove your theories," his opponent countered triumphantly.

"I leave that to lesser scholars," Barry said acidly.

"My dear sir," the white-haired man protested, growing red in the face, "are you implying that..."

We pretended to listen to the 'discussion' at the table, though in reality I was closely watching my surroundings, trying to familiarise myself with as many faces as possible. Since research scholars, dependent mainly on the massive school library, also stayed at the castle on a permanent or semi-permanent basis, I needed more information on the people present.

Fortunately, a woman with long blonde hair, who must have been around my age, was quietly eating her vegetables only a few seats away. She was following the discussion, though appeared to be too reserved to participate herself. She was wearing a polite face, though she clearly disliked the increasingly hostile insults being hurled across the table.

"Excuse me," I said, leaning over to her. "Could you tell me who that warlock is?"

I pointed to the man arguing with Barry.

"Oh, that's Professor Olsen," she said, grateful for the distraction. "He's my boss, actually. Are you assistants to the Earl of Barrington, then?"

"That's right," I said, trying to suppress a grin at the mention of Barry's official title.

It wouldn't do, of course, to start a discussion on the inheritance of Fickleton House. In fact, it was probably best to omit that little detail altogether. My relationship with Barry would have to appear purely professional – not familial.

"My name is Esther, by the way, Esther Hickey," she said, smiling pleasantly and extending her hand.

"Nice to meet you," I said, shaking it. "I'm Amanda Sheridan, but just call me Amy. And this is Val."

"Hi," Val said, "I'm also assistant to Barr–"

I quickly kicked her foot under the table.

"– I mean, the Earl of Barrington."

"Is it true that he got himself trapped in that cat's body?" she asked curiously.

"Yes," I said. "Quite true. That was long before our time, though."

"We wouldn't have let that happen to him," said Val, nodding earnestly.

"Poor man," said Esther. "It must be horrible."

"Don't worry, he makes the best of it," I said, thinking of the way Mrs. Faversham doted on him at home.

"That's very brave," she said. "I'd very much like to meet him. I've been an admirer of his work for some time. Apart from therianthropy, he's written some very insightful articles on water magic, too. Part of my research transcends the border between earth and water magic, you see. Professor Olsen is the head of the earth magic department. Do you have a focus yet?"

"Erm, no," I said, not untruthfully, "I've just started out really. But the... Earl of Barrington has allowed me some time to think about it."

"That's certainly very gracious of him," Esther said, sighing. "I wish I had had that."

"What do you mean?" I asked.

But at that moment, the discussion had blown up into a shouting match, and we were no longer able to ignore it.

Professor Olsen, no trace left of his urbane academic stutter, was on his feet, pointing his finger angrily at Barry.

"Your work is nothing more than idle speculation," he shouted, shaking from head to toe.

"Better speculative than derivative, *professor*," Barry countered, jumping onto the table. "your life's work is nothing more than the summary of others' research."

"I will not listen to these lies," Professor Olsen screamed. "LIES, do you hear?"

And, with a dismissive gesture at the world around him, Professor Olsen kicked away his chair and stormed away. Stunned, we all watched him go down the aisle, his wild hair flying all around him, and exit through one of the side doors of the Great Hall. Still furious, he banged it closed behind him as hard as he could.

For a moment, the Great Hall was silent. Then, a few students laughed in bewilderment, and everyone returned to what they were doing previously. Barry, who seemed to interpret the unexpected turn of events as nothing less than a full-scale rout of his opponent, returned to slurping his stew from his bowl.

I turned around to Val and Esther again. If I wasn't mistaken, there was something akin to fear in Esther's eyes. Perhaps this hadn't been the first time that Professor Olsen had exploded.

"I…" she began, but faltered.

Then, she began to hyperventilate, her eyes widening in an unmistakable attack of anxiety.

"Esther, I'm sorry," I said, trying to calm her. "The Earl of Barrington is rather… pugnacious at times."

"It's… it's not that," she whispered. "Never mind. Sorry, I didn't want to bother you with…"

She was in such a state of nerves that she knocked over the glass of water in front of her. Helping her mop it up with my napkin, I said:

"Don't worry, it's really not a bother."

"You're very kind," she said, trying to smile. "I think I had better get back to my work. Thank you for being so kind."

Wiping away the remnants of her tears, Esther got up and briskly crossed the platform. She exited through a small door that I hadn't noticed before.

"So much for gathering information," Val said ironically. "We'll be lucky to find out anything before Barry starts a civil war in this place."

"I wonder what she was upset about, though," I said, staring at my now empty plate.

"Well, they were shouting at each other, you know," said Val. "Some people prefer a little harmony from time to time."

"Could you tell that – psychically, I mean?"

Val shook her head.

"Sorry, Amy," she said. "The only way I can survive with hundreds of people in one room is to shut it out completely. Otherwise, I'd go crazy. But if we get her on our own later, I'm sure I could read her."

"Good idea," I said.

Out of the corner of my eye, I saw a familiar figure enter the hall at the far end. It was the headmistress. The look on her face told me that something was seriously wrong. She scanned the staff table from afar, catching my eye almost immediately. Then, thinking it was probably too obvious to approach me or the table directly, she jerked her head ever so slightly toward the exit, turned on her heel, and left the hall again. Her meaning couldn't have been made any clearer, however.

"Excuse me a moment," I said as inconspicuously as possible. "I just remembered, I think I left something upstairs."

Val, unfortunately, hadn't seen the headmistress at all and was rather at a loss. But before she could inquire, I pointedly raised my eyebrows at her, my back turned to the other people at the table.

"Oh, alright, Amy," Val said, her voice slightly higher than normal. "I'll see you later then."

An ominous feeling in my stomach, I walked as fast as I dared towards the main exit of the Great Hall. We had only been at the school for a few hours now. What could have possibly happened?

Luckily, nobody around me seemed to be taking any notice at all. The students I passed were still as loud and as boisterous as ever.

Shutting the heavy oak doors behind me, I spun around to find the headmistress standing next to one of the hideous waxwork figures they kept in the antechamber of the Great Hall, herself almost as motionless and pale as the figure, a 16th century witch standing in front of a cauldron.

The headmistress's eyes, however were wide awake and fearful.

"Miss Sheridan," she whispered. "Another sign has just appeared. I think you need to see this for yourself. Please, come with me immediately."

CHAPTER 5

Without another word, I followed her. Despite her usual apathy, I was surprised at how fast Muriel Hall could walk in her present state of mind. But perhaps it was precisely the nervous energy that provided her with the temporary strength to do so.

Once more, we passed along the many corridors and chambers of the castle. It had struck me before that there were no windows at all, neither in the Great Hall nor in any of the corridors leading to it. In fact, I had only ever seen the outside world in the headmistress's office through the large windows behind her desk. Most of the school, I surmised, was probably deep underground.

At last, we reached what looked like a dead end. But the headmistress pulled out her wand and waved it with a quick flick of her wrist. The massive stone wall in front of us rumbled and vibrated for a second. Then, an archway formed, just high and wide enough for us to pass through, vanishing as soon as we had stepped over the threshold.

On the other side, a long flight of steps led downward. The portraits and waxwork figures had vanished completely in this part of the castle. Though I didn't mind the absence of the waxworks, it looked a lot less cared for than the areas I had seen so far. I was able to smell the moisture all around me.

We reached a chamber with a small, metal door with bars on it. The headmistress stopped and said:

"This, Miss Sheridan, is what was formerly known as the dungeon. Today, it is mainly used for additional storage."

Passing through, we found ourselves in a long passageway lit by torches, with slits in the walls at either side that overlooked what must have been – at some point in the past – cells. Finally, the headmistress came to a halt in front of another metal door.

"It… it is in here," she said, pulling herself together as best she could. "Clement should also be on his way. I had a student search for him immediately. We'd better go in. Come with me, please."

She reached out for the handle and pulled. Beyond, there was nothing but darkness. I took out my wand from my own handbag and lit it, peering into the room. It was filled with an assortment of boxes, empty bottles, disused bird cages, and odd pieces of wood. As I entered, I noticed that the ceiling was very low, so that I could barely stand upright. The smell of mould was almost unbearable.

"We rarely use this room anymore," the headmistress said unnecessarily. "Most of the items you see are rarely used. Though from time to time, we do need something. The sign is over there, next to the old wardrobe."

The wardrobe's doors were so dilapidated that they were almost crumbling to pieces in front of our eyes. The dark paint that covered it was gradually peeling off due to the damp.

"There," the headmistress said, her voice quivering slightly. "The mark of the necromancer."

My eyes wandered slowly from the wardrobe to the area next to it. For one insane moment, I didn't want to look at it, but I forced myself to do so all the same. Painted on the wall in a bright green colour, three skulls leered at me, their hollow eye sockets as dark as the wall behind it. Above, a white staff towered over the skulls.

My heart started racing. In itself, I tried to tell myself, the sign was hideous, though really not harmful. And yet, as I continued to look at it as though I were prey mesmerised by a predator, the awful history that was connected to it suddenly seemed to speak to me in this moist dungeon. The necromancer's sign – and therefore the danger – was real, but the consequences were still frighteningly uncertain.

What exactly had happened to the missing people was left to the horrible scenarios my imagination was conjuring up, though I had very grave doubts about whether they were still alive.

I looked away, trying to pull myself together again. I was letting myself get carried away, sucked into and frozen within the horror. I couldn't let that happen. People were depending on me. I had to remain rational, even though every inch of me felt like running away.

Gazing back at the sign, I stepped forward to examine it more closely. I could see by the clots of paint that it had been both a hasty and an unprofessional job. Undoubtedly, however, judging from the lack of dust and the moist surface, it was quite fresh. Strangely, the skull on the left had been smudged, most likely with something like a cloth or a towel.

"When were you informed of this?" I asked, examining the smudged paint more carefully.

"Quarterwarlock Armbruster notified me, only minutes before I came to you," she said. "He reported it straight away."

"I suppose he didn't see anyone?"

"He did," the headmistress said. "A student was caught in this very room, but claims to have nothing to do with it."

"Who is this student?" I asked.

"A girl called Isabella Villar. She's an exchange student from Spain. She's something of a troubled soul. As they often are at that age, I suppose."

"So you don't think her capable of kidnap and murder?" I asked.

"It is hard to believe, but, as I said, no one is beyond suspicion."

"Well," I said, "she might have painted it herself. This looks very fresh to me."

"Yes," the headmistress said, "it's certainly possible. Oh, Miss Sheridan, this is all so *horrible*. Suspecting everyone

around me. I didn't know I'd be dealing with this sort of thing when I took the job."

She paused, closing her eyes as if to shut out the awful reality of her situation. Her breathing was fast, close to hyperventilating. Then, she puffed up her cheeks and exhaled very slowly.

"Please forgive me, Miss Sheridan," she said, after a minute's silent breathing. "It's just… you see, this particular sign… the one with the three skulls and the staff… it always preceded a disappearance."

"How much time do we have?" I asked.

"A few hours, a few days, I think – I hope – that was how it was in the old days, when Wycliffe was still at large."

White in the face, she sat down on one of the boxes close to her, her breathing becoming shallower again. Her makeshift seat was full of cobwebs and dirt, but she was far too worried to care.

"I'm very sorry, headmistress," I said. "I promise I will do everything in my power to get to the bottom of this."

I meant it. Slowly, abstraction was being replaced by grim reality. And with lives at stake, we had to put an end to this once and for all.

"Thank you," she said, with a much steadier voice. "That is very kind of you. How would you like to proceed?"

"I will need to talk to the student in question – Miss Villar," I said. "Perhaps I can squeeze out some more information. It's our only lead so far."

"I will make the arrangements," she said.

"Is there some quiet space I could use?" I asked.

The headmistress paused briefly.

"Well, there's my office," she said, "but you could also use the Earl of Barrington's office. We've provided him with a spacious room in the West Tower. Close to your sleeping quarters, in fact."

"That sounds excellent," I said. "I think we will question her there, straight away. Could you also ask the quarterwarlock, Mr. Armbruster, to come along, too?"

"Of course, Miss Sheridan," she said, her face returning to a healthier colour. "I'll have Clement arrange everything for you. And let me just say, once more, how grateful I am for your help. It really means everything to this school."

***

An hour later, I found myself with Barry and Val – who had stayed in the Great Hall during my excursion to the dungeons – in Barry's new office. I had quickly filled them in on what had happened. Val had jumped at the idea of interviewing Miss Villar and Mr. Armbruster, while Barry had only reluctantly consented after some persuasion.

Though not quite as large as the headmistress's quarters, Barry's office was indeed very spacious. It also sported large windows, though the view was not of fields and meadows but, as far as we could tell from the light of the moon, of rocky slopes leading further up a hill.

"You can't see *anything* out of these, just a few rocks hanging over your head," Val was saying. "I mean, what's the point?"

"We must be close to mountains," I said. "Where exactly is the school located, then?"

"A secret location," Barry said unhelpfully.

He was sitting at his desk, already in his element as visiting scholar and esteemed lecturer. Wearing his reading glasses, he was leafing through loose pieces of paper containing his notes, which he said he needed to prepare for the coming days. Next to them, several stacks of books covered the rest of the table's surface.

"That's not very specific, Barry," Val said. "Give us a hint? Surely, you of all people must have some idea of where we are?"

Once again, flattery had done the trick. Barry looked up, taking off his glasses with both paws.

"Naturally. I think we are in Wales somewhere," he said. "Judging from the landscape, I'd say we are in Snowdonia, though not quite at the highest peak, of course. The school is under English jurisdiction, however. I remember quite clearly that in 1957 there was some debate about…"

We were saved from Barry's spontaneous lecture by a sudden knock on the door. Since it was Barry's office, he answered. It was peculiar somehow to see him in a position of real authority for a change. Though, unsurprisingly, Barry didn't have a hard time adapting.

"Yes?" he said curtly.

The door opened. The deputy headmaster, his blond hair as slick and his smirk as superior as ever, came in first. He was followed by a very heavy man with a red beard. He was wearing what looked like an apron a smith might wear in his workshop. Behind him, a girl with dark hair, dressed in black clothes from head to toe, entered, also. Apparently, the magical world was not spared the idiosyncrasies of teenage clothing habits.

"I see you have made yourself comfortable, my lord," the deputy said, hardly able to conceal his sneer.

"Yes, yes," Barry said, enjoying himself as gatekeeper. "What do you want?"

Deputy Harper's eyes flickered briefly towards me.

"You wished to speak with quarterwarlock Armbruster and Isabella Villar, I believe?"

"Quite right," said Barry. "You may go."

It was hilarious to see Barry bossing around the deputy headmaster, but since we were there by the headmistress's express wishes, there was little he could do. He looked daggers at all of us and then left the room without a word.

"Have a seat," Barry said to Mr. Armbruster and Miss Villar.

Both found it neither odd nor unusual at being addressed by a cat sitting at a desk. Perhaps, some teachers preferred to remain in animal form, or accidents like Barry's were not so uncommon in the magical world as I had previously supposed. In any case, they both sat down on the chairs in front of Barry's desk. We had elevated Barry's own chair to the maximum level, so that he was now towering over them, like a judge in a trial. We had agreed beforehand that Barry would start the questioning, as it was simply the more plausible beginning than if his research assistant led the way.

"Quarterwarlock Armbruster, could you tell us how you found Miss Villar?" he asked.

"Well," Armbruster said, locking his huge hands in front of his oversized belly, "it was in the storage room, down in the dungeons."

"Did you see Miss Villar draw the sign on the wall?" Barry asked.

"No," he said slowly, "but I did see a light inside. That's what made me go there in the first place, because I was only passing through. But when I opened the door, she quickly extinguished her wand light."

"I see," said Barry. "I understand there have been other drawings of these signs. Has anyone else been caught in the act?"

"No, my lord," he said, "not that I am aware of, anyway."

Barry looked across to Val and me, inviting our questions. I grasped at the opportunity immediately.

"Mr. Armbruster," I said, "how often do you go to the dungeons?"

"In that particular room?" he said, stroking his black beard with his hand. "Not much at all, really. It's old and useless stuff in there, most of it."

"And how often are you in the dungeons, generally?" I asked.

"Every other week, perhaps," he said. "I keep some of my equipment in there."

"I understand," I said, "that certain ingredients have

been stolen from the school's supplies. Is that correct?"

"That's right," he said.

"Would it be possible to compile a list for us, with times and dates of when you noticed that they had gone missing?" I asked.

"Yes, of course," he said. "I've kept records. I'll get on it right away."

"Thank you," I said. "That would be most appreciated."

I nodded to Barry, who said:

"Yes, that will be all, Mr. Armbruster."

But the quarterwarlock didn't move. He eyed the girl sitting next to him with deep suspicion. Then, he turned back to us.

"Are you sure that…" he began.

"Quite sure, thank you," I said.

"Alright," he said. "I'll be in the Great Hall for a nightcap if you need me. I'll deliver the list to your office then, Lord Barrington."

Barry inclined his feline head in gratitude. We waited briefly for Mr. Armbruster to leave before questioning Isabella Villar. I was just about to start when I remembered what the headmistress had told me. Nobody was to be trusted at Warklesby's School of Magic.

I quietly stepped over to the door to make sure Armbruster was gone. My instincts, as it turned out, hadn't failed me. As I opened the door, Armbruster was just a little too late in pretending to walk down the corridor. Had he been trying to eavesdrop on the conversation we would be having with Isabella Villar?

"Oh, erm, is there anything else you want?" he asked innocently.

"No, Mr. Armbruster, nothing else."

"Right, I'd… I'd better be off, then."

"Yes, goodbye," I said.

I stood there, watching him. There was nothing else for him to do but turn around and walk away. Once he was safely around the corner, I came back into Barry's office. Val and Barry hadn't, it seemed, started asking questions yet. Before we proceeded, I suddenly had an idea. Rummaging for my wand in my handbag, there was one extra precaution I wanted to take.

"Barritha!"

Shooting out of my wand with a whoosh, a sound-proof glue spread across the office door. You're not really paranoid if they're really out to get you, I thought to myself. I'd certainly be watching Mr. Armbruster very closely in the upcoming days.

Now, however, there was the more pressing matter of Isabella Villar. You didn't have to be a psychic to tell that this office was the last place that she wanted to be at the present moment. She kept fidgeting with one of her bracelets, looking anywhere but directly at us. Matching her black clothes and dark hair, she had opted for a heavy layer of makeup that I was sure was several shades lighter than her actual skin colour.

"Miss Villar," Barry began pompously, "I hope you appreciate your difficult position. Drawing a forbidden sign – the sign of the necromancer, no less – is in itself punishable by magical law."

Isabella Villar gulped but didn't say anything.

"As you undoubtedly know, however," Barry continued, "there is a lot more at stake currently at the school. People have been disappearing. And there is good reason to believe that they may have been killed."

For the first time, Isabella Villar spoke. She had a slight Spanish accent.

"I had nothing to do with this," she said.

"What *were* you doing down in the dungeons?" I asked.

Isabella Villar paused briefly, as if considering her answer very carefully.

"I wanted something from the storage room," she said.

"What did you want?" I asked.

"I needed new phials," she said quickly, though I thought it sounding slightly rehearsed, "for my alchemy lessons. I knew that there were some down there."

"A strange place to look," said Barry suspiciously "Why didn't you acquire some at the school store, like everyone else?"

"I have no money," she said. "Nobody uses those old things. Nobody would have cared if... if..."

"... if you hadn't drawn that sign on the wall?" said Barry harshly. "I think not."

Isabella Villar grew red in the face with indignation.

"I did not do that," she said, raising her voice. "I did not!"

"Perhaps," I said, trying a different tactic, "Miss Villar was indeed at the wrong place at the wrong time."

She looked surprised.

"However," I continued, "it is important that you also see our perspective. You do want these disappearances to stop, don't you?"

"Of course," she said. "I... I knew Robert. Everybody wants this to stop."

"Then you must help us," I said. "If you are innocent, then help us to move on. Every minute spent on the innocent is a moment that the guilty party can breathe freely. So, I ask you again: what were you doing down in the dungeons?"

"I told you, I was looking for bottles."

"I thought you were looking for phials?" Barry said triumphantly.

"Yes, that is what I meant," she said. "Phials for alchemy class."

"Mr. Armbruster saw you standing next to the sign of the necromancer," I said. "The phials were nowhere near there. Tell us the truth, Miss Villar: If you have any compassion for those people, tell us what you were really doing."

She opened her mouth, but no words would come out. She was looking furiously at all of us. And yet, I could see that I had struck a nerve somewhere. Instead of saying anything, she suddenly pulled back her left sleeve. Her fingers were covered in green paint, the same paint that was used for the sign of the necromancer.

"So," Barry said, "it *was* you."

"No," I said, remembering the smudged skull. "You tried to wipe it away, didn't you?"

"Yes, I did," Miss Villar said proudly.

"But Mr. Armbruster caught you before you could get rid of it?"

"Yes," she said.

"Why did you try to wipe it away?" I asked.

"It is a sign of evil," she said. "Bad things follow whenever it is drawn."

"Do you know who put that sign on the wall?" Val asked, getting up from her seat and walking over to Barry's desk.

"No," she said flatly. "I do not."

I wasn't quite sure whether to believe her or not. Barry, evidently, was thinking along the same lines.

"Tell us the truth, Miss Villar," he said sternly. "If you know the person who drew the sign, give us the name."

But it was to no avail. However hard we tried, we had met a dead end. Whatever she knew, she wouldn't say anything further. Finally, Val placed a hand on Barry's fur, signalling that there was no point.

"Let her go," Val said.

"What?" Barry spluttered.

"She has told us all she knows," she said.

Barry looked aghast from Val to me. I didn't know what was going on, but I trusted Val's instincts. I nodded briefly. Barry, still perplexed, finally said:

"Fine, Miss Villar, that will be all – for now. Report straight back to your dormitory. I would advise you not to wipe away any more signs. They may be of vital importance."

"What is my punishment?" she asked icily.

"That is not for us to decide, Miss Villar," I said. "All we want is to know what happened to the missing people. If you remember anything – anything at all – please don't hesitate to contact us here. We will make sure it remains confidential. I promise."

Miss Villar hesitated briefly. Then, she nodded, got up, and headed straight for the door without another word.

When he was sure that she was safely out of earshot, Barry turned on Val.

"Are you mad?" he said. "She obviously knew more."

"I agree," said Val. "But she wouldn't have told us anything."

"And why not?" Barry asked angrily. "A few more minutes, and I could have cracked her."

"I felt her emotions, Barry. They were strong. Very strong. There is no way in a million years that she would have talked. She's covering up for somebody. Somebody very close to her."

CHAPTER 6

"Who is she covering up for?" I asked Val. "Could you tell?"

"No," she said. "All that I know is that she is very loyal to this person. I sensed her fierceness. If we want to find out who it is, we'll have to do it some other way."

"I'll have the headmistress put her under house arrest," said Barry, who was still incensed by being lied to.

"No," I said. "How are we going to find out who she is covering up for if we do that? Val, do you think Miss Villar will warn whoever drew that sign?"

"If that person is still at the school, I'm sure of it," said Val. "With such strong feelings, it would be the most natural thing to do."

"The sooner the better, most likely…" I said. "If I were in her shoes, I'd do it quickly, wouldn't you? I mean, you don't know when you'll get another chance. You might be questioned for the next week, for all you know. Necromancy is no joke. Miss Villar knows that."

"But we can't watch her day and night," said Barry irritably. "She could slip that person a note, or leave a message somewhere. Or whisper in someone's ear in the Great Hall with hundreds of people talking at the same time."

"It's certainly a daunting task," I agreed. "All I'm saying is that we should keep an eye on her."

"Well," said Val, "Barry would be best suited for that. He can hide pretty much anywhere."

"I've got better things to do than to spy on teenagers," Barry protested. "Look at all these notes! I've got a lecture to prepare."

He gestured towards the sheets of paper on his desk.

"We'll take it in shifts, then," I said. "It's our only lead so far."

"Fine," said Barry impatiently, "but first I need a good night's rest before tomorrow's class."

***

Reluctantly, Val and I agreed. It had been a tiring first day at Warklesby's School of Magic, so any more detective work would have to wait for the morning, when we could make a fresh start.

We left Barry snoring in his little bed, situated on a mezzanine right above his desk. He couldn't climb the slippery metal rungs leading up to it, however, so I had conjured up a cat ladder for him instead. I was getting quite adept at creating feline furniture by now.

Val and I, meanwhile, were to sleep in a small dormitory – only a few flights of stairs away from Barry's office – that was reserved for outside researchers and guests. The dormitory was small, with no more than ten rooms perhaps, but it featured a communal area with comfortable sofas and a fireplace, where the last cinders attested to a fire having been lit a few hours earlier.

At the other end of the room, a group of waxwork figures depicting several hooded warlocks and witches in black robes sent waves of ice down my spine. In the dim light provided by the candles hanging on the walls in the common room, they looked eerily alive and human. I would definitely make sure to lock myself in tonight. Judging by the look on Val's face, she felt just the same way.

We found our names on a door label at the very back, tucked away behind a corner. The room had two beds, a wardrobe, two chairs, and a table. Adjacent to it was a bathroom. It wasn't luxurious by any standards, but it would certainly do for a few days. Fresh towels and linen had been provided for. Fortunately, our bags had already been brought up, too.

The room was stuffy, however, so we opened the window at the back immediately.

"At least it *has* a window," said Val, slumping down on one of the beds. "The rest of the castle is so dark with just torches. And what's with the wax statues all over the place? Like in a horror movie, or something."

"Yeah," I concurred, thinking longingly of Fickleton House's cosy and – most importantly – waxwork-free hallways. "They are well made, though. Some real craftsmanship."

"That's what I'm afraid of," said Val. "They probably magicked them to jump at you when you're not looking."

I laughed.

"Come on, Val, it won't be for long."

"I hope so," she said earnestly. "This place gives me the creeps, Amy. Something horrible is going on, I can sense it. It's in the air, if you know what I mean."

After trying to reassure Val, both of us made ready for bed. It was still very warm inside the room, though the light breeze coming through the window certainly helped. After a good shower, I put on my nightgown and slipped into bed. Val followed shortly after. We said goodnight, and I extinguished the candle on the table with my wand.

Neither of us, however, could sleep. After tossing around uselessly for a few minutes, I could hear Val turn around in the darkness.

"Amy," she said, "do you think we've met the necromancer yet?"

"I don't know," I said. "We haven't met all that many people."

"I'm still betting on the deputy headmaster," said Val. "Nasty person."

"He certainly is," I said. "What about the headmistress, though?"

"Muriel Hall?" said Val in disbelief. "Well, if it's her,

she's certainly hiding it well."

"It's happened before," I said slowly.

"What about that Mr. Armbruster?" said Val.

"Certainly a shifty character," I said. "Listening at doors makes for a suspicious pastime. Did you feel anything with him."

"I'm not sure," said Val. "Isabella Villar's emotions were so strong, she made his appear rather blurry. I did feel that he was a bit on edge, though. But some people simply are like that."

"A bit like Professor Olsen," I said, thinking of his spectacular clash with Barry in the Great Hall. "He seemed to fly off the handle pretty quickly. Esther – his assistant – seemed to be downright afraid of him."

"Yes," said Val slowly. "And whoever is doing this is taking a sadistic pleasure. I mean, it's not just that people are being abducted, but all of these signs are designed to create an atmosphere of fear."

"Yeah," I said. "Anyway, we should suspect everyone until we have evidence to the contrary. Might turn out it's a student, even."

There was a moment's pause.

"Amy?" said Val.

"Yes?"

"D'you really think Wycliffe has come back from the dead?" she asked.

"I don't know," I said again. "Seems quite convenient for our kidnapper, though, don't you think? You can just blame it on a dead sorcerer."

We discussed the different possibilities for an hour or so longer, though we knew that it was all conjecture. It felt good to talk about it all the same. With our need to find the proverbial needle in the haystack, guess work provided a form of solace.

Exhausted from the events of the day, we finally fell into a deep yet uneasy sleep.

***

A few hours later, I was awoken by what I thought was the wind howling outside. Groggily, I wiped my eyes, opening them. It was still pitch black. Val was snoring next to me.

I couldn't check my phone for the time, since the magical energies surrounding us in the school prevented it from working. I lit my wand for light and got up, walking over to the window.

Closing it, I was just about to climb back into bed when, once more, I heard the mysterious noise that had awoken me. It couldn't have been the wind after all, I thought.

I stood still, listening for it again. And then, sure enough, it returned. It sounded human, though I couldn't be sure. If I wasn't quite mistaken, it wasn't coming from outside at all but from inside the walls.

It felt silly to wake Val for no reason. It might just be my imagination playing tricks on me, a result of the talk we had had before we fell asleep. But curiosity was gnawing away at me, egging me on to find out the sound's origin. And, I reasoned with myself, I could easily call for Val if it was anything serious.

Extinguishing my wand, I wedged it into the sash of my nightgown. You couldn't be too careful with a sorcerer on the loose.

I unlocked the door and stepped into the common room, which was still lit by the weak light of the candles, though – miraculously – they hadn't burnt down even an inch.

Pricking my ears up, I waited, trying to locate the sound. Vaguely gazing at the dormitory's exit, something bright glinted in the corner of my eye. Had something moved nearby?

"Who's there?" I spoke into the empty room, spinning

around and drawing my wand.

But there was nothing there – except for the sinister waxwork figures that had so repulsed me earlier. Standing in a group of five, the faces beneath the hoods were as unrecognisable as ever.

My wand hand shaking slightly, I inched closer, watching for the slightest movement, fearful that they might jump at me at any moment.

And yet, they remained perfectly still. But as I approached, I saw the glint of light again. One of the figures, a warlock at the back of the group, was wearing a gold signet ring on his left hand. The candle light must have been reflected in it.

I lowered my wand. Feeling rather foolish, I was just about to go back to bed when I heard a door open and the patter of naked feet behind me. I was half expecting to see Val. Instead, a slender figure had appeared, barely visible in the darkness.

"Who… who's there?" a woman asked, her voice sounding oddly subdued yet familiar.

Screwing up my eyes, I finally recognised her. It was Esther Hickey, the researcher I had met in the Great Hall earlier. She looked terrible. Her face was red and blotchy, while deep bags under her eyes suggested she hadn't slept at all.

"I…" I began, not knowing how to explain myself. "Sorry, I thought I heard something outside. Those waxworks… well, I…"

"Oh, them," Esther said, wiping what I suspected to be the remnants of tears from her left cheek. "One gets used to them eventually."

"Is… is everything alright?" I asked, trying not to sound overly intrusive.

"Oh, it's nothing," she said, "just…"

She looked at me for a while, evidently making up her mind whether to tell me or not. Then, without further warning, she burst into tears.

"I-I'm s-sorry," she spluttered, holding her hands to her face. "I just can't stand it anymore…"

But she tailed off before saying anything more. She closed her eyes, teetering dangerously on the spot. Afraid that she might faint on the spot, I tried to stabilise her with my hand around her waist.

Slinging her arm around my neck, I moved her over to the sofa at the fireplace. She had closed her eyes, hardly responsive to what was happening around her.

"Would you like something to drink?" I asked her.

With what seemed like extreme effort, she opened her eyes again.

"S-so sorry," she murmured.

"Esther, would you like some water?" I asked.

Feebly, she nodded her head. Careful to leave her so that she wouldn't fall from the sofa, I hastened over to my room. Val was still snoring peacefully in her bed. We had a few glasses in the bathroom, courtesy of the school, which would have to do.

Returning with a clean glass of water, I pulled the door to our room shut, careful not to wake up Val, and went to Esther with the glass of water.

Raising her head with difficulty, she drank it gratefully. When she had emptied the whole glass, she looked at me and attempted a smile.

"Thank you, Amanda," she said. "That's very kind of you."

She handed me the glass, which I placed on a nearby table.

"Rough night?" I asked, sitting down on a nearby armchair.

Esther lowered her eyes.

"You could say so," she said. "It's just… just so much pressure. Professor Olsen…"

She broke off again, though I could see she was bursting

to tell someone.

"Do you promise not to breathe a word of this to him? Or anyone else, for that matter?"

"Of course," I said.

"I don't want them to think I'm a complainer," she said. "It's just got to a point where, well... where I don't know what will happen next."

Esther looked into the fireplace for a moment, as if she were miles away.

"He's not a very nice man, you see," she said finally. "Professor Olsen, I mean."

"How come?" I asked.

"Well," she began, struggling to find the right words, "I don't know why exactly. But ever since I arrived here as his assistant, he's so... irritable. Angry, often for no reason at all. Starts yelling uncontrollably."

"And he takes it out on you?" I asked.

"Yes," she said softly. "Not only me, though. His secretary gets most of it, I think. And there's the other assistant – Hubert Metcalfe – with whom he argues a lot, too. I've talked to Hubert, and he's just as puzzled as everyone else."

"So, this is a recent change in him, then?" I asked.

Esther nodded her head emphatically.

"Absolutely," she said. "I'd never have come back here otherwise. I was a student of his for the last few years at Warklesby's, you see. I did my exams with him and everything. He told me he was always on the lookout for good researchers and asked me to join his team. And so I did."

"Very strange," I said. "Do you know when exactly this change occurred?"

Esther shifted uncomfortably on the sofa.

"Now, I don't want you to understand this the wrong way. It's likely – no, most certainly – a complete coincidence. But it all started with these mysterious disappearances at the school. At the time, I wasn't back again at Warklesby's yet, but the secretary – Mrs. Kettle – told me all about it.

"He changed," Esther continued. "And pretty quickly, too. As a student, we had got on very well. I'd seen Professor Olsen at meetings and gatherings plenty of times. I even had private lessons with him. He guided me in my research, helping me gain an understanding of earth magic that certainly transcended the normal school curriculum. He was almost like a father to me, academically speaking."

She brushed a thin strand of hair behind her left ear.

"But when I finally arrived here as a researcher and assistant – so glad to be back at the school I had loved as a pupil – Professor Olsen was dismissive and downright rude. It was almost as if he couldn't remember who I was or just didn't care. He didn't even afford me my own quarters in the department of earth magic, so I've had to use this dormitory instead. I see my colleagues only during mealtimes, and I'd be completely in the dark if Hubert and Mrs. Kettle wouldn't keep me in the loop."

"That sounds horrible," I said sympathetically.

"It is," Esther said grimly, though her voice was now much steadier. "According to Mrs. Kettle, Professor Olsen changed right about the time people went missing and when those horrible markings started appearing all over the school."

"Do you think he might have anything to do with it?" I asked, deciding not to beat about the bush.

Esther stared at me for a minute, as though uttering the words tempted the universe to make it true. But I could see that the possibility had been haunting her. What had initiated the strange and sudden change in Professor Olsen's behaviour? Had he simply been particularly unnerved by the strange disappearances at the school? Or was there perhaps another, a darker reason?

"No," she whispered, her eyes so wide I could see the

white all around her irides. "I just don't… whatever reason would he have to do that?"

"I don't know," I said. "Can you think of anything at all that has changed?"

She paused, staring at me for a moment while she considered her answer.

"Well, there is… one thing that struck me as very strange. Professor Olsen was always a prolific writer, producing several books and dozens of articles a year. Yet according to Hubert, he hasn't produced anything new for quite some time. He only has Hubert rehash some of his old works."

"Perhaps he has lost interest in his subject?" I said.

But Esther shook her head.

"That's the strange thing. He locks himself up in his laboratory for hours and hours. It's certainly not to prepare his lectures, either – he could do those in his sleep after so many years. The truth is that none of us really knows what he gets up to in there."

"Where exactly is his laboratory?" I asked.

"The department for earth magic is in the East Tower. Professor Olsen's laboratory is at the top of the tower."

"Thank you for telling me," I said. "I know it's very difficult for you."

"You won't tell anyone, will you?" she said, panic in her voice. "I wasn't insinuating anything, I… I just needed to talk to someone. It gets pretty lonely in this dormitory."

"Don't worry," I said. "Your secret is safe with me."

Relieved, Esther smiled and slowly lifted herself up from the sofa. She was still rather uneasy on her feet, but much better than before. Looking relieved, it was almost as though she had cleansed herself of a great burden by merely speaking of it.

I was getting very tired myself. Professor Olsen's strange behaviour was certainly worthy of further investigation, though it would have to wait for the next day.

Supressing a yawn, I escorted Esther back to her room. It was even smaller than ours and had no window at all. Books, journals, newspapers, and pencils seemed to cover every inch of it.

"Thank you again," she said. "I hope the Four Druids of Lutetia don't bother you again."

"Sorry?"

"The waxworks in the common room," she clarified, smiling.

"Oh," I said, laughing. "No, I hope not. Well, goodnight."

"Goodnight."

I stepped outside and closed the door behind me. I was feeling very groggy now. I was just about to go back to bed when something about Esther's words struck me.

The *Four* Druids of Lutetia?

I was certain I had counted five earlier on. Whipping out my wand – wide awake again – I stepped over to the hideous waxworks.

To my shock, Esther was right. There were only four hooded figures. The one with the ring that had caught my eye earlier was missing. Someone, disguised as a waxwork, had been listening in to every word we had said.

CHAPTER 7

The next morning, as I hurried along Warklesby's many corridors after a few hours of snatched sleep, my sense of growing paranoia in regard to the waxwork figures didn't improve, considering that there seemed to be one in every corridor of the castle.

During a hasty breakfast, I had told Val and Barry all about my talk with Esther and the disturbing thought of someone posing as a waxwork, secretly listening to our conversation.

"But," Val had said, a note of pleading desperation in her voice, "couldn't you have just made a mistake with the waxworks? It must have been dark, and we *were* very tired when we came to the dormitory."

"I told you, Val," I had answered, "I remember it clearly. Also, none of the four druids had a ring the second time around. There was someone else there, I know it."

***

Barry's first lecture was to take place in a hall not far from the East Tower. Neither Val nor I were particularly keen on attending, though in the interest of our cover – as assistants to the Earl of Barrington – it was vital to keep up the performance for as long as possible.

When we arrived, the hall – shaped like an amphitheatre – was buzzing with the noise of pupils talking and laughing. As far as I could tell, they were older students, probably in their senior years. There was also a great deal of unauthorised magic going on, though most of it seemed to be good-natured pranking. Surprisingly, Julian Ross, who had been in trouble with the headmistress only the previous day, was not involved. Instead, he was sitting in the front row near the door, clearly lost in thought, with no trace left of his usual cocky smile. Perhaps, I thought, Headmistress Hall had been able to talk some sense into him after all.

Val and I sat down at the assistants' table, next to the blackboard, facing the crowd of students. I conjured up a glass of water for each of us.

At last, Barry made his entrance. Wearing a tiny black gown that covered most of his fur, he had donned a square academic cap to match. Val and I had to supress a giggle as he haughtily walked towards us.

"What is it?" he hissed.

"Nothing," I said quickly, well aware that some of the students in the front row were paying close attention. "Your notes are ready for you on the table."

Barry leapt onto a high stool that we had placed behind his lectern. Due to the lack of sufficient light coming in through the high but narrow windows in the hall, he turned on the green reading lamp next to his bowl of milk, which we had brought up specially from the kitchens. A magical microphone ensured that he could be heard by everyone present.

"Welcome," Barry said, his voice reverberating around the hall, "to my lecture series on the many complexities and intricacies of therianthropy. I am pleased to say that Warklesby's School of Magic has made ample room for them, however, in what I hope will truly be an enlightening first five-hour session."

"*Five* hours?" Val mouthed at me, a look of horror on her face.

I gulped but said nothing. We were in for one long lecture by Barry. With no escape in sight, Val and I had no other choice but to surrender to the present circumstances.

***

Two and a half hours later, Barry finally looked up from his massive stack of notes and announced a break. It was like awakening from some sort of trance, which had been both anaesthetising and informative at the same time.

Val, for whom the magic was of less interest, was still in a near-comatose stupor. I prodded her gently, and she shook herself visibly, wrenching herself back into the present.

"Have… have I missed it?" she said.

"Don't be so optimistic, Val," I said softly. "Still half way to go."

"Oh," she said, "we'd better attend to Barry, then."

Barry, however, was surrounded by inquisitive students who had flocked to the lectern to pose him some questions. My gaze moved toward the rest of the crowd, which was drifting lazily towards the exits. Then, near the door, I spotted a familiar face.

"Look, Val," I said, pointing, "isn't that Isabella Villar over there?"

Val squinted her eyes for better vision.

"You know, Amy, I think you're right."

"How long is the break, do you know?" I asked.

"Only about twenty minutes, I think," said Val. "Why?"

"Well," I said, turning around conspiratorially to make sure that we couldn't be overheard, "she won't be seeing the person she's covering up for now, then. But we should remain vigilant, all the same."

"Yes," Val said, "but what about Professor Olsen's lab?"

"I thought we might poke around there later this afternoon. I checked his timetable, and he's got class at the other end of the castle then. It should give us enough time. If we get out of here alive, that is."

"Come on, Amy, you shouldn't be too hard on Barry. He's having the time of his life," said Val, grinning.

At that moment, Barry's voice was clearly audible from beyond, ticking off an overly eager student for his patent ignorance.

"Clearly," I said drily. "Only problem is that we have to deflate his head when we're back home."

"It might be permanent this time," said Val, just as a pair of senior female students giggled at one of Barry's snide yet accurate comments. "We'd better catch the culprit quickly."

"You bet," I said, laughing.

***

'Quickly', however, became a relative matter the longer the second half of the lecture went on. But I noticed that I wasn't the only one who was restless. I had scanned the crowd for Isabella Villar and found her sitting at the very edge of the back row, close to the aisle. Every minute or so, she looked at the large hourglass hanging on the wall. Fidgeting with the notes she was supposed to be taking, Isabella Villar seemed desperate to escape the lecture hall as soon as possible.

Surreptitiously, I pointed this out to Val.

"Should we follow her?" asked Val, leaning over to me.

"Wouldn't hurt," I whispered.

Finally, Barry's lecture came to an end. The avalanche of information had clearly left its mark on all present. The more ambitious students – sitting mostly in the front row – had amassed what appeared to be short novellas in terms of notes. Yet, even those who had been less keen were clearly physically and mentally worse for wear.

Unfortunately, a large group of students had congregated around Barry's lectern, asking follow-up questions. Under the pretext of gathering his lecture notes, I bent down so that nobody else could hear.

"We're tailing Villar. Meet you later."

Unsurprisingly, Barry played the role of professor perfectly. Turning his feline head, his hat tipped slightly to one side, he nodded.

"Thank you, Miss Sheridan, just put them on my desk. I will see you in my office later."

Supressing a smile, I agreed and swiftly scooped up the rest of the notes, conjuring up a black suitcase with my wand in order to carry them all.

The students were now streaming out of the exits. Val – no doubt on Isabella Villar's tails by now – was nowhere in sight. Joining the fray, I navigated my way through the crowds until I was clear of the lecture hall.

In the corridor beyond, I spotted a less than inconspicuous Val at the far end near the archway that eventually lead to the Great Hall, waving to me from the spearhead of pupils streaming along like some gigantic snake.

Before I could make any progress, however, I heard a faint yet distinct call next to me.

"Amanda. Amanda, over here."

It was Esther Hickey. She looked quite different from last night. She seemed excited, though the urgency of her voice indicated to me that it was something important.

Val, meanwhile, was still desperately trying to get me to hurry up. I motioned her onward with both of my arms and mouthed 'go on', though I think it was eventually the torrent of students that broke the dam that was Val standing in the archway. She had no choice but to swim along. I only hoped that she would be in time to follow Isabella Villar.

Luckily, most of the students had passed by me, so I was able to follow Esther to the wall so that we couldn't be overheard so easily.

"Is everything alright?" I asked.

"Yes," she said, lowering her voice, "I mean, no – well, it's about Prof. Olsen. I can't explain here. You'd better come with me to the laboratory immediately."

"OK," I said, with a last glance in the direction of the

lecture hall where Barry was no doubt still besieged by students. "Lead the way."

We hurried along, passing quite a few students who were headed for their next class or the Great Hall for tea. Though I didn't have any means to tell the time in the mostly windowless corridors, I reckoned that it was probably afternoon already.

A few minutes later, Esther came to a halt in front of a large door with a brass handle.

"This," she said in a soft voice, "is the East Tower. The department of earth magic is here. The laboratory is at the top."

The wooden flights of stairs leading upwards were surprisingly narrow, owing to the rather low diameter of the tower. What it lacked in width, however, it made up for in height. The steps seemed endless and excessively steep, so that more than once I stumbled and almost fell into Esther. Though only very few students came out of the classrooms that led off of the stairs – earth magic did not seem to be a favourite – inching past one another on creaking boards required some serious manoeuvrability.

At last, we had reached the top of the tower. I could tell that Esther was still nervous, though she seemed much steadier than the night before. We found ourselves on a circular staircase with a balustrade all the way round.

"This entire floor is dedicated to the laboratory," said Esther quietly.

"Is... is Prof. Olsen here?" I asked, gazing around.

"That's the peculiar thing," said Esther. "He sent a note to his secretary this morning, saying that he had an urgent appointment and had to leave immediately. Hubert was tasked with taking over his classes. I... I thought it would be the perfect opportunity to have a look around the laboratory."

"Good thinking," I said. "Did he say why he had to leave so suddenly?"

"No," Esther said, shaking her head. "He's quite secretive. But he usually gives the secretary some way of contacting him in case of an emergency. Apparently, he didn't do that this time. He said he didn't want to be disturbed."

"Very suspicious," I agreed. "If he is involved somehow, we need to find out as soon as we can. How much time do you think we'll have?"

"I don't know," she said. "But he had packed a large bag, according to Hubert, who met him in his office before he left to discuss the classes. That would mean he was staying the night, wouldn't it?"

"Perhaps." I said thoughtfully. "Or he might be transporting something."

"Should we go back?" she asked.

"No," I said, drawing my wand. "We might not get another chance."

Esther hesitated briefly but finally nodded. She produced a large stack of keys from her pocket and began trying them one by one.

"I borrowed these from the secretary's desk," she said. "Must be one of them. I've seen Professor Olsen use them."

"Can't we simply magic it open?" I asked.

"No," Esther said. "There is a powerful spell to prevent that. These are magically protected locks. Ah, here we are."

The door swung open before us. We were dazzled by rays of sunshine that pierced the large windows beyond, making us hold our hands to our eyes. From this high up, the view of the surrounding rocky hillsides and forests was magnificent.

Carefully, we entered the room, which wrapped itself round the staircase from which we had entered. Every inch of the laboratory was covered with magical instruments of all types and sizes. Several tables were stacked with mysterious powders and phials filled with dark fluids I didn't recognise. Scraps of papers with indecipherable formulae littered the walls.

Backed against the wall at the laboratory's right side, a blackboard was covered with strange symbols and runes. Next to it, a potion was simmering in a cauldron above a magical fire. Evidently, Professor Olsen wasn't planning on staying away for too long. Placed at the wall, various cardboard boxes were stacked close to a small table.

"Is there anything out of the ordinary?" I asked Esther, who knew more about earth magic than me.

"Well," she said, approaching the blackboard. "I'm not sure what he is working on. Most of these things are related to the school curriculum, though. Pretty standard. He must have his own research somewhere else."

I decided to leave her and investigate the rest of the laboratory, to the left from the entrance. It turned out that it was devoted mostly to storage, with countless shelves containing all sorts of plants, metal objects, and fine instruments. Various crates of different sizes and a solid stone wall marked the end. Inside the crates, I found mostly commonplace ingredients for potions.

Slightly disappointed, I made my way back to Esther. She was still standing in front of the blackboard with the same confused expression on her face.

"I'm sorry, Amanda," she said. "I just don't understand. This is almost as if… as if something is missing. It doesn't make any sense at all. I haven't found any original research at all."

"Perhaps it's in here," I said, turning to the small table behind me and trying to open its stubborn drawer. "Though it will probably take hours to get through these."

"Oh, I'm just hopeless," Esther said miserably. "I'm sorry I brought you here, Amanda, I don't know what I was…"

But at that moment, in a move that would have even Val blushing, I must have exerted a bit too much force, for the drawer came clean out of the table, sending me flying to the ground. I was showered in paper, while an ink bottle went zooming through the air. But instead of hitting the wall behind the table, it suddenly disappeared.

"Hold on," I said, gingerly getting to my feet. "Did you see that?"

"No, what is it?" asked Esther.

"It's the ink bottle…" I said.

I thought perhaps the ink bottle had simply dropped onto the table, but there was nothing there.

"Help me with this, will you?" I asked, indicating the table.

Together with Esther, I carried it out of the way, so that we could reach the wall directly behind it. I moved my hand slowly forward until it was only an inch away from the wall. Then, as I was about to touch it, the tips of my fingers vanished before my eyes.

"Ingenious," I said.

Esther seemed somewhat shaken, so I stepped in first. I found myself in a pitch-black room. None of the light penetrated the secret magical wall through which I had entered. It smelt of something foul in here, and the heat was almost unbearable.

Muttering the incantation as softly as I could, I lit my wand. For a moment, I was dazzled by the bright beam. But as my eyes adjusted, I found myself in a small, rectangular room. The walls were covered with newspaper cuttings and pictures. Many of them, however, had been torn down. The floor was covered not only in paper but also broken glass and stinking liquids. Shelves had been smashed or cleared of their contents. It looked like a battleground.

Raising my wandlight, my eyes followed the trail of waste until, to my horror, I spotted a figure at the far end of the room, sitting on a chair, completely motionless.

Suddenly breathing very quickly, I grasped my wand tightly in my wand hand.

"Who are you?" I demanded.

There was no answer.

Esther, who had followed me inside by now, grabbed my arm in panic. Slowly, I edged forward, with only the cracking of glass underneath my shoes to break the eerie silence.

As I got closer, there was no mistaking the shock of white hair.

"Professor Olsen!" Esther screamed.

We hurried across to him immediately. But it was too late. Professor Olsen was already dead.

CHAPTER 8

Esther muffled a scream with her hands. Feeling a sudden rush of anxiety myself, I pointed my wand shakily around the room. But there was nobody else there except for us, neither person nor waxwork. Esther and I were alone.

Careful not to touch anything, I shone my wandlight onto Professor Olsen again. There was a burn mark on his right temple. His right hand was dangling down, still clutching a wand. It had wooden carvings that ran counter to the fingers.

"Th-this is so horrible," Esther said, staring at Professor Olsen's lifeless body as though transfixed by a snake. "Do you think he might have t-taken his own life?"

"It certainly looks that way," I murmured.

I bent forward, examining the burn mark more closely. It was blacker in the middle, with sharp red streaks at the edges. I had never seen anything like it before.

The desk in front of Professor Olsen was untidy, stacked with papers and notes. The many stains and remnants of powders on the wood attested to the fact that Professor Olsen had used this room many times in the past. Flanking the desk on either side, shelves held yet more phials containing poisonous-looking substances, while others had also been tossed to the floor.

"Esther," I said softly, "I need you to get help immediately. Please tell the Earl of Barrington that we need him here. He should be in his office. I don't think Val will be there, but if she is, tell her to come, too. After that, please inform Headmistress Hall of what has happened here. Can you do that?"

With difficulty, Esther tore her eyes away from the body

and nodded. She took out her own wand and, with one last horrified glance at the dead man in the chair, turned around and exited the secret chamber.

Now alone, I needed a moment to pull myself together. There was nothing to fear, I said to myself, though the corpse right next to me told me otherwise.

Trying to distract myself, I began examining the newspaper articles on the wall next to the entrance. It seemed that Professor Olsen had had a keen interest in reports of necromancy, both in general ("London Necromancy Ring Exposed"), as well as at the school itself ("EXCLUSIVE: Is Warklesby kidnapping linked to necromancers?"). Here and there, key words and phrases were underlined. The sensationalist articles seemed to contain little more than speculation, featuring the occasional 'expert' interview.

On the opposite wall, the newspaper clippings were older. Most of them concerned the terror at the school many years ago, as well as the arrest and trial of Wycliffe. Despite the yellow paper and fading colours, Wycliffe's deluded gaze was still frighteningly life-like. He had blond, greasy hair that almost reached down to his shoulders. His gaunt face had high, prominent cheekbones and an unusually thin mouth that was no more than a slit when he sneered at the camera. His piercing grey eyes betrayed no inkling of remorse.

Moving away from the press cuttings, I stepped closer to Professor Olsen's desk again. Notes were pinned to the wall all over the place, though I could see that many had been ripped off and scattered upon the table. Strange markings and complicated calculations were scribbled on them. Although it was difficult to tell, the contents of his research looked a lot different from the ones outside. Perhaps there had been a reason why Professor Olsen had decided to keep these particular works in here, away from prying eyes of colleagues and students.

***

After a harrowing quarter of an hour or so, Barry arrived at last. He was wearing a very serious expression indeed and, for once, did not moan about having to climb up the many stairs of the East Tower. Esther wasn't with him, but she had apparently explained the exact location of the secret entrance to him.

"Where is he?" he said.

"Over here," I said.

Approaching the Professor Olsen's lifeless body, Barry nimby jumped onto the desk – careful not to disturb anything – in order to examine the dead man.

After several minutes in silence, Barry seemed satisfied.

"It was the killing curse alright," he said. "No doubt about it. Close quarters, as you can tell by the characteristic burn marks."

"Was it suicide?" I asked.

"Probably."

I was just about to turn around when a familiar glint caught my eye. Professor Olsen's other hand was resting on his lap. It was wearing a gold ring. A ring, in fact, that I was sure I had seen not too long ago.

"Barry, look!" I said excitedly, pointing at it. "I've seen that ring before. In our common room. On the fake waxwork figure I told you about at breakfast."

"Curious," Barry said, his whiskers twitching.

"*He* must have been the one eavesdropping on me," I said. "His stature certainly fits. I'd say he's about the same size as the waxwork figure."

"Then the only question remains," Barry said, "of why Professor Olsen wanted to spy on you and his assistant in the first place. He must have got wind of our investigation very fast. Not that one had to be a mastermind to figure that one out, I suppose."

"He already knew," I said, remembering what Headmistress Hall had told me. "He's on the school board. That's what Muriel Hall told us when we arrived. She said that she would ask him not to tell anyone."

"Yes," said Barry slowly, "that certainly explains his speed."

"What do you make of these drawings?" I asked Barry, indicating several scraps of paper on Professor Olsen's desk.

Barry carefully navigated the messy desk to peruse them. After a moment, he grunted, moving on to the next piece. At last, he seemed satisfied.

"What do you think?" I asked him.

"It's necromancy alright," said Barry. "No doubt about it. If I'm not mistaken, this is part of a plan for a resurrection."

"You mean, of a human?" I asked, horrified.

"Yes," Barry said. "And have a look at these maps. I'm almost certain that they show the school grounds. Yes, these are the woods, you see? He's marked them out for some reason."

Barry pointed at a large green area with several clearings. A thick red circle was drawn around the entire forest. Next to it was a question mark.

"I wonder what he was looking for?" I said. "It's not very specific, is it?"

"I don't know," Barry said thoughtfully. "Have you noticed anything else of interest?"

"Have a look over there," I said, pointing to the wall to the right of us. "Looks like Professor Olsen was something of a Wycliffe fan."

Barry leapt down from the table and strutted over to the wall containing the newspaper clippings and began to read some of the reports.

"Calling this an obsession would certainly be an understatement," Barry said drily. "Looks like we've got our man."

"The evidence seems to point that way, I suppose," I said, frowning.

"You aren't convinced?" said Barry. "What more evidence do you need?"

"Well," I said, pacing the room. "It's all a little too perfect, don't you think? I mean, here we are, looking for a necromancer. And then we just happen to come across a secret office full of Wycliffe press clippings and how-to manuals for necromancy. A sick mind intoxicated with Wycliffe's crimes, a professor certainly capable of complicated and advanced magic. But the necromancer himself is dead, conveniently killed by his own hand."

"Are you telling me this was staged, Amanda?" Barry said, raising his eyebrows.

But before I could retort, two people entered the secret chamber. It was Deputy Headmaster Harper, followed by a frightened-looking Esther.

"There has been a death?" Harper said unnecessarily.

"Where is the headmistress?" I said, irritated to see him.

"I'm sorry, Amanda," Esther began, "I couldn't find her…"

"Headmistress Hall," Harper said, an unmistakable smirk of triumph on his face, "has unfortunately been delayed on her trip to London. She is currently liaising with MLE officers. In the meantime, *I* am in charge of investigations. And you will answer to me. Now, step aside so that I can examine the body."

His cold eyes scanned the position of the body, the burn marks, and then the wand in Professor Olsen's right hand. After that, Deputy Harper perused the newspaper clippings, as well as the notes on the desk.

"So that is what he was up to," Deputy Harper breathed. "I should have known…"

He looked at Professor Olsen's body with disgust. Then he turned around to me with a peculiar look on his face.

"It appears we have all underestimated you, Miss Sheridan. The culprit has been revealed to be Professor Olsen. I will inform the MLE immediately, as well as the headmistress."

Without another word, he strode towards the exit.

"I don't think it was him," I said before he reached the magical barrier.

Deputy Harper turned around as if a bothersome fly had just started harassing him.

"What did you just say?" he said.

"I don't think Professor Olsen is the man we're looking for."

"Your evidence?" Deputy Harper said curtly.

"Well," I said, unwilling to say that it was more of a hunch than anything else, "the room, for one. It's a mess. There might have been a fight, or a search. Both of which suggest that there's more to this."

"And who, pray, searched the room?" Deputy Harper sneered, disbelief etched across his face.

"The person who killed Professor Olsen," I said. "He could have rearranged the body quite easily."

"But you *do* realise, Miss Sheridan, that this is Professor Olsen's own laboratory, do you not? These newspapers are not here by accident," he said, gesturing towards a particularly striking picture of Wycliffe on the wall. "Or did this mysterious killer also change the décor after he finished brawling with his victim?"

Feeling my anger rising, I took a deep breath in order to avoid exploding on the spot.

"Deputy Harper," I said, speaking as calmly as possible. "The main question is why Professor Olsen would kill himself if he was the guilty party? It doesn't make any sense."

"Do not ask me to understand the mind of a criminal maniac," Harper spat. "Perhaps the necromancer had a moment of clarity and did the only decent thing left to him, destroying much of this room in the process."

"But what about the people who were abducted?" I said.

"We will find them eventually, if they are alive, although I highly doubt that to be true."

"But…" I began.

"The case," Harper said, his eyes narrowing dangerously, "is closed. I have heard quite enough of this nonsense. And I am sure that Headmistress Hall will concur as soon as I have had a word with her. You will cease all further investigations immediately."

CHAPTER 9

The news of Professor Olsen's death spread like wildfire. This was, perhaps, unsurprising given the fact that Deputy Harper had made very little effort to keep it a secret. Professor Olsen's body had been removed from the secret chamber and was being inspected by experts from the MLE. They didn't even want our testimony.

By the time we were back at Barry's office, darkness had already fallen. I was still fuming at Harper's patronising ignorance, but I was also dying to tell Val everything that had happened.

Fortunately, we found her snoozing on the sofa, an open book entitled *Psychic Signs and Symbols* in her hand. As we approached, she drowsily lifted an eyelid.

"Amy?" she said, yawning. "What's up?"

Settling down on one of the comfortable armchairs next to her, I told her the entire story, from how Esther had tipped me off to Deputy Harper's entrance.

"I must say," Barry said pompously after I had finished, "that Professor Olsen's morbid fascination with necromancy doesn't surprise me in the least. Awful fellow. Always knew that there was something sinister about him. Just couldn't quite put my paw on it."

"Oh, come on, Barry," I said. "You just didn't like him because of your squabble about theory the first day we got here."

"Well," Barry puffed indignantly, "of course I didn't know he kept a secret cabinet full of reports on Wycliffe, but there was *obviously* something wrong with him. I mean, who in their right mind would solely rely on Farthing's outdated theorem? Utterly absurd."

"So," Val said, ignoring Barry's last point, "was

Professor Olsen really a necromancer, then?"

"He was certainly fascinated by Wycliffe and necromancy, that's for certain," I said. "But there's something wrong about this whole thing."

"Oh, dear," Barry said in a mock-weary voice, "here we go again with the conspiracy theories."

"What conspiracy theories?" Val said.

"I don't think it was suicide," I said. "It doesn't make any sense. A necromancer who has spent years, if not decades, working on all this stuff, compiling his little cabinet all in secret, suddenly decides it's not worth it anymore?"

"Perhaps someone found out," Val said.

"Maybe," I said. "But Olsen did tell his staff that he was going away. I mean, he could have just destroyed the evidence and run for it."

"Well, what do you think happened?" Val asked.

"My guts tell me that he was killed, and the murder was staged as a suicide to end the investigation. Deputy Harper was quite keen to do just that, if you remember."

"Is there any way to tell if it was murder or suicide, Barry?" Val asked.

"Not if they used his own wand against him," Barry said.

"And that would most likely only happen after a scuffle," I said triumphantly, "which perfectly explains the mess the room was in."

Val pondered on this for a while, but Barry's tail was waving to and fro in irritation.

"Even if you're right, Amanda, you still have to account for the fact that Olsen was eavesdropping on you, disguised as one of the waxwork figures. It would be hard to explain if he wasn't the necromancer."

"He must have had another reason, then," I said, though I was at a loss myself in that regard.

"So if Amy's right," said Val, with a shudder, "then the

necromancer – who is also the killer – is still roaming the corridors of the school."

"Perhaps," Barry said, "we should consider the motive more thoroughly."

"Maybe Professor Olsen was a rival necromancer?" Val said. "Or maybe he knew too much and had to be silenced."

"Yes," I said, "that would make sense. But who did it?"

"I bet that awful deputy headmaster has something to do with it," Val said. "He's been trying to end our investigation the moment we arrived."

"It could be someone closer to Professor Olsen," said Barry. "After all, they had to know about the secret chamber somehow."

"You mean, a member of his department?" I asked.

"Precisely," he said. "Who do we have there?"

"Well, there's the secretary and the assistant I haven't met yet," I said. "And there's Esther, too. But she doesn't really strike me as the necromancer type."

"Don't be fooled by a good performance," Barry said. "Remember that it was Esther who led you up there in the first place. That might be more than just a coincidence. Valerie hasn't been able to penetrate the culprit's mind – if he or she is still out there, that is. But so far, it's all guesswork."

"Then what we need most," said Val, all matter-of-fact, "is to keep poking around. If Amy is right, and the necromancer is still on the loose, we can't just sit around."

"Agreed," I said.

Barry was about to protest, but quickly thought better of it after seeing our determined faces.

"Alright, alright," he said. "Have it your way. But don't blame me if it turns out to be Olsen all along."

"So," Val said brightly, "where do we start?"

"Any luck with Isabella Villar?" I asked her. "That's our only other lead."

"Oh, that's all under control," Val said, leaning back. "She's ill. That's what a girl in her class told me. Been in her room all afternoon."

"She's ill?" I asked suspiciously.

"Yeah," Val said.

"Did you actually check the room?" I asked.

"Well," Val flustered, "not exactly. I was tired and…"

"Val!" I exclaimed.

"I was waiting for you," she said apologetically.

"Do you know where her room is?" I asked.

"Sorry, Amy, I was going to find out tomorrow," said Val miserably.

"Where is the students' dormitory?" I asked, turning to Barry.

"Amanda," Barry said, "Warklesby's has over a thousand students. There is no one single dormitory. But there is a general registry where we can find out where she is."

"Illness my witch's hat," I said. "There isn't a minute to lose. Come on."

***

Despite hurrying along the now deserted corridors and chambers of the castle, I felt that our best opportunity may have already slipped away. Of course, we might simply find her in her room, as she had claimed to be. But something about her timely illness told me that there was a very good chance that Isabella Villar was not where she pretended to be.

After half an hour, we reached the general registry next to the students' office, which was close to the Great Hall and the main entrance.

"There it is," said Barry, pointing to a massive book that was chained to a table. "She should be in there. It's updated every semester."

It turned out that it not only contained the present inhabitants of the school, but also all who had ever attended over the course of the many centuries it had been in existence. Finally, we were able to track her down.

"West Tower, bottom floor," I said, making sure I hadn't slipped a line. "Villar, Isabella."

"Wonderful," said Barry bitterly, "we could have just gone downstairs."

"Yeah, well we didn't know that at the time, did we?" I said.

"This body can only take so much," Barry whined. "What I need is rest and relaxation."

"Oh, stop moaning, Barry," I said, grinning. "You'll get your brandy soon enough."

Barry's complaints notwithstanding, we raced back the way we had come as quickly as we could. Though I didn't want to agree openly with Barry, running up and down endless flights of stairs was indeed quite taxing. I only hoped that it was not in vain.

As we finally reached the student dormitory in question, we were completely out of breath.

"D'you think she's in?" Val whispered.

"I don't know," I said. "But there's only one way to find out. We can't just wait around here, doing nothing."

"Right," said Val.

"You two'd better wait here," I said. "Otherwise she'll think it's suspicious."

"What will you say if she's there?" said Val.

"Oh, I'll think of something," I said.

Isabella's room was at the end of the corridor. I knocked on the door. Immediately, I heard the scampering of feet inside. A moment later, the door was opened. But it wasn't Isabella.

Instead, a girl with black braids and a sour look on her face answered the door. She stood in the frame, eyeing me with suspicion.

"Yes?" she said, without smiling.

"I'm looking for Isabella," I said. "Do you know where she is?"

"She in trouble?" the girl asked.

"No," I said evasively, "not exactly. But there's something important I need to see her about."

"Get in line, then," the girl said, pulling a face.

"Do you know where she is?"

"I might," she said, looking me up and down. "Depends who's asking."

"Look," I said, deciding that honesty was the best policy. "My name is Amy. I'm looking for the people who've disappeared. I think Isabella's in trouble. Deep trouble."

"She's got nothing to do with that," the girl said defensively.

"I know, but I think she might be able to help us," I said. "Please, tell me where she's gone."

The girl stared at me for a while.

"You promise this won't get her into worse trouble?" she demanded.

"I promise. Quite the contrary, in fact."

The girl nodded.

"I'll take your word for it. She's gone to meet someone in the woods. She wouldn't tell me who it is. There's a hut, deep in the woods, but don't ask me where it is. That's all I know."

"Thank you," I said.

"Don't tell her that I told you, though," the girl said quickly. "She'll be mad. Real mad."

"Yes, of course," I said gratefully. "Thank you again."

***

"Wait," Barry said. "Are you saying that..."

"We should follow her right now," I said. "Come on,

there isn't a moment to be lost."

"But," Barry spluttered again, "but it's almost midnight! I've got a class tomorrow and…"

"It can wait, Barry," said Val. "Amy's right. It's now or never."

He mumbled something that sounded a lot like 'brandy' and 'sofa', but left it at that.

***

"You know," Barry said, as we approached the gates that led out into the school grounds twenty minutes later, "I didn't realise that detective work included so much running around. Next time, I'll just stay in my office."

"Perhaps we should make a habit of taking brooms with us," Val said. "Could be a time-saver."

"Brooms aren't safe for cats, you know," Barry said. "We tend to fall off."

"Only because you insist on talking all the time, Barry," said Val.

"Shh, you two," I said. "Let's keep our eyes peeled for Isabella."

Unfortunately, the gates were shut tight. Even my trusty unlocking spell couldn't do anything to remedy the situation. Luckily, however, we found another side entrance, tucked away in one of the adjacent corridors. It led to a wooden storage room.

"Looks like a tool shed or something," said Val, looking around her.

"Strange that this is unlocked, though," I said.

"The quarterwarlock is in charge of this, I believe," said Barry, careful not to step on any of the rakes that were resting against the wall.

"What does a warlock need spades for?" asked Val. "Couldn't he just dig with his wand."

"Enchanting a spade is easier," said Barry. "Or any

other tool, for that matter. Especially if you're planning a larger operation."

"Hope he's not around," said Val. "That man gives me the creeps."

"Yeah," I agreed.

Then, there was a loud creak and a thud, as though an old door had just been closed in the distance.

"Did you hear that?" said Val, swerving around.

"There's nobody here," said Barry, though he didn't quite believe it himself, "there can't be. Not at this hour, at any rate."

"Come on," I said. "Better keep moving. I think this door might lead outside."

I pushed it open as gently as I could. Through the crack, moonlight streamed into the shed we were in. I poked my head through the opening, checking the surroundings outside. A lawn extended for a few hundred yards, with dark woods looming ominously beyond it. Isabella was nowhere to be seen. There was no cover from the surprisingly bright moonlight out here, however. If anybody chanced to look out of the window, they'd most certainly be able to spot us.

We crossed the open space as quickly as possible without breaking into an outright run. Although I turned around multiple times in all directions and saw nothing, I just couldn't help the feeling that we were being followed.

When we finally reached the edge of the woods, we all sighed in relief. Though finding Isabella would be more difficult in the woods, we would be harder to track down as well.

"It's so dark," Barry protested. "How are we supposed to find anything in here?"

"You're a cat, aren't you?" I said, exasperated. "You should be able to spot her from a mile away."

"My eyes are tired, I've been reading all evening," he said. "And I can hardly see through all these ghastly trees anyway, can I?"

"We'd better stick to the path," I said. "For the time being at least. Have you ever been in here before, Barry?"

"Certainly not," he said. "Nor do I wish ever to return."

"Fine," I said, losing patience. "Stay here if you want. Come on, Val."

Grudgingly, Barry trotted after us, though he kept his eyes open for any movements from now on. The minutes streamed by without any hint of Isabella Villar, though I wished by now that I had brought a coat with me. It had been warm enough, of course, during the day, but the nights seemed to be a lot chillier here than at Fickleton House.

Tired and frustrated, I was just about to recommend that we go back when Barry stopped in his tracks. Something in the distance had caught his eye. Val had noticed it, too.

"What's the matter?" I whispered.

"Over there," said Barry. "I can't be certain, but it looks like a hut of some kind."

"That must be the one Isabella's flatmate mentioned," Val said excitedly.

"And I'm sure I saw something move, too," Barry said.

Leaving the path, we stumbled across leaves and branches, with Barry leading the way. The trees were so thick that, though I trusted Barry, I could hardly see where my own feet were going.

"I think I can hear something," Val said softly.

We stopped, listening intently. She was right. Though very faint and muffled, the noises were undoubtedly of human origin.

"Amy, can you cast that silencing spell on shoes, too?" Val asked.

"Good thinking," I whispered, drawing my wand.

Barry, of course, didn't need it, so I cast the spell for Val and myself. It was a peculiar sensation, as though walking on gel, but it was certainly effective. Now, we were able to approach without a sound.

Finally, I saw the outlines of the hut from the little moonlight that was able to penetrate the treetops. I was also able to make out specific words now. It sounded as though the voices were arguing.

"Told you… just stupid…" a female with a familiar Spanish accent was saying.

We were close to the hut now, within throwing distance. Inside, two shapes were moving about, clearly agitated. I signalled for Barry and Val to wait, while I crept closer to the window that was nearest. It had no pane. Crouching in the earth beneath, I could now hear every word that was being uttered inside.

"Why," Isabella was saying angrily, "why do you have to do that? So foolish. If you get caught, there will be no hope for you left. They asked me questions after questions about the mark. They *know* I lied. I can't protect you if you continue like this."

There was silence inside the little hut. I didn't dare move in my hiding place, though I was dying from curiosity to know who the other person in the room was. But the conversation didn't continue. Instead, I saw the two shapes embrace. All of a sudden, I felt like I was intruding in something very personal. There was only way to find out who it was.

I stood up and lit my wand, shining the beam through the window. The room inside was illuminated immediately. Isabella Villar, her face frozen in horror, jumped back and almost fell onto the floor. But my eyes raced to the other person in the room. To my utter amazement, it was a face I had seen not too long ago.

CHAPTER 10

It was Julian Ross.

Barry and Val had joined me at the window, too, and were now staring in disbelief at the unlikely couple inside of the hut.

"Ross?" I said. "Julian Ross?"

As in the lecture hall, he had lost his cheeky swagger from our encounter in the headmistress's office entirely. Instead, his face white as a sheet, he was opening his mouth and closing it again like a fish. It was Isabella Villar, therefore, who took control of the situation and went on the offensive.

"How dare you spy on us like this?" she said. "You should be ashamed."

"Perhaps," I said, "that is true. But from what the little I heard, I think Mr. Ross here has a lot more to be ashamed of."

Isabella Villar was at a loss for words now. I pressed my advantage as best I could.

"There are two possibilities open to you both," I said. "Either you come clean, right here and right now, or I will have to report you to the headmistress and the MLE. But to be honest, I think expulsion from the school will be the least of your worries then, Mr. Ross. You will be facing very serious charges indeed."

Isabella Villar turned on Julian Ross.

"Julian," she said, "you must tell them."

"No," he said quietly. "I won't. It's pointless."

"Please," she said, grabbing his hand. "Please, do it for me."

"They won't believe a word of it," he said, shirking away.

"OK," Isabella said, turning around to face us, "then I will. I will tell them everything you did. If you are too stupid to save yourself, someone else will have to do it. And if not your girlfriend, who else?"

Val opened the door to the little hut, and we filed into the crammed space within. There were no chairs and only a rotten table in the corner, so we just stood there, looking at each other for a moment.

"Tell us," I said to Isabella, "about the necromancer's sign. The *whole* story, this time."

Julian Ross shifted uncomfortably on the spot, watching his girlfriend closely. But he was beyond protest. The game was up. And yet, I felt, the circumstances of his deeds would prove decisive.

"Julian drew the mark on the wall," Isabella said. "We had been quarrelling about it. I said that I would go down there myself and get rid of it. And so, I went to the dungeons."

"But before you could wipe it away, Mr. Armburster, the quarterwarlock, caught you?" asked Val.

"Yes," she said.

"Why did you draw the mark, Julian?" I asked him.

"You won't believe it anyway," he said sulkily, so unlike his former boisterous self.

"Why don't you try me," I said.

But he remained silent, looking out of the window instead, through which the moonlight shone into the little hut. For a moment, I thought I heard a noise outside. Or had it simply been the whooshing of the wind?

"I trust you don't want to go to prison?" Barry asked Julian Ross.

"Of course not," the latter said at once.

"We are interested mainly in the people that are missing," Barry said, pacing up and down in front of Julian and Isabella, "as well as solving the mystery surrounding Professor Olsen's death."

"That's right," I said, walking slowly towards Julian. "We don't care so much for the marks as for the disappearances. And, whatever else you are, Julian, I don't think you are capable of kidnap or murder."

He looked up in surprise.

"You see," Isabella said, turning on him, "I told you that they are different. They're not just looking for a scapegoat, as you always say."

"Why," I asked, "did you draw that sign, Julian?"

"Well, isn't it obvious?" he said, his nostrils wide. "They're all so complacent. The MLE was at the school, what, how many times was it? Five times? Guess what they did. Absolutely nothing. NOTHING."

He was suddenly shaking with rage. But at least he was finally talking.

"Robert, my best friend, was the first to go missing," he said, his voice cracking, "but everyone just assumed that he had run away, though I knew that that wasn't like him at all. I... I started seeing Isabella here in the woods. She knew him too. But one day – it was dark, much darker than now – I lost my way. I must have taken a wrong turning when I left the road. The hut isn't far from the road, as you know, but I walked for hours and hours and couldn't find it. I was beginning to panic. Well, at some point I was just about to give up and sleep under a tree when I heard voices nearby. I thought perhaps that someone from the school had come looking for me, perhaps even Isabella, so I walked in their direction. But as I came closer, I noticed that they were singing or chanting. At first, I thought they'd be able to help me."

He stared at all of us as though the next part was too horrible to relate. But the touch of Isabella's hand on his shoulder seemed to enable him to press on.

"As I got closer," he continued, "I saw that there were two people wearing thick, black robes with hoods over their faces. They were in a wide clearing with three large trees in the middle of it. They were standing around a stone. Something was on it, but I couldn't see what it was at first. Up close, I realised that they weren't really singing at all. It seemed to me more like they were trying out some sort of complicated channelling spell."

"Can you remember what it was?" asked Barry, his face very serious.

"No, not the words exactly," he said. "But as I moved closer, I saw that the thing on the stone – which looked more like an altar – was a third person, just lying there. And… and on the ground, there were bodies of animals around it… I…"

But he broke off, unable to utter anything more than a croak.

"What sort of animals were they?" I asked patiently.

"S-snakes," he said after a little pause. "Lots of them. That's when I started to panic. I hate snakes, you see, always have, even at the zoo. Then, I tripped and fell into the bush next to me."

"Did you recognise the third person, lying down?" asked Barry, who was wearing a very grave look on his face.

"No," said Julian, "no I didn't."

"What happened then?" I asked.

"I don't know whether they had heard me fall, or maybe something went wrong, but they suddenly stopped their chanting. In any case, they were in a real hurry. They levitated the figure off the altar and were gone before I could do anything. "

"And what did you do after that?" I asked.

"Well, I waited for the sun to set and also to make sure that they didn't come back. I hid behind a tree that had fallen down. When I was sure that the coast was clear, I stepped into the clearing. Among the snakes, I also found… I found a watch."

"A watch?" Barry asked, bewildered.

"Yes, a wristwatch. I recognised it immediately. It

belonged to my best friend, Robert."

"But I thought they don't work around magic," I said, frowning.

"They don't," said Julian, "but, you see, Robert wasn't born a warlock, he inherited his skills. He had been very fond of the watch as a heb so, even after it stopped working at Warklesby's, he just continued to wear it."

"Did you have any idea of the nature of the ritual you had just witnessed?" Barry asked.

"I guessed," said Ross, "but I wasn't sure until later, that the animals meant something very sinister. I think they had practised their spells on them first. In the library, I flicked through book after book until I found confirmation of what I had seen. It took me ages to do it. But finally, I found out that what I had seen was some sort of necromancer's ritual."

"That sounds horrible," said Val.

Julian nodded.

"It was even worse that the school authorities and the MLE weren't on the right track at all. I decided to paint the walls of the school with the mark of the necromancer, so that they would understand what they were dealing with."

"Why didn't you tell them about this?" I asked.

"I did exactly that," he said, his face contorting with righteous anger. "That was the first thing I did. But they just said I was cooking up trouble and that they didn't believe a word of it. They said that *I* had planted the watch there, for all they knew, and had invented a tale around it. They said that I wasn't coping with the loss of my best friend. The only one who seemed to believe me was Professor Olsen."

"Professor Olsen?" I said, staring at him.

"Yes," said Julian. "He tried to talk to them, but it was no use. He questioned me about the whole thing several times. Wanted to know every little detail."

"Mysterious," I murmured.

"They left me no other choice but to draw attention to the truth by drawing those marks," said Ross stubbornly.

"Who were *they*?" I asked. "Who did you talk to?"

But before he could answer, the door of the hut suddenly flung open with a crash. In the doorway, deputy headmaster Harper was standing with his wand pointed at Julian Ross. Harper's slick blond hair was unusually untidy, thin strands dancing on his forehead.

"He told *me*, Miss Sheridan," he said, a malicious smile on his face. "The whole pack of inventions and lies. That's when I knew I'd have to watch him more closely. I'm surprised you listened for as long as you did. You have been wasting your time with Ross."

"But I told you," Julian said, red in the face, "it's the TRUTH."

"Don't you dare lie to me again," Harper hissed. "You have committed nothing but mischief at this school from the moment you set foot in it. Do you expect me to believe you after all that?"

"But... but this is different," Julian spluttered. "I'm telling you, this is what happened. Necromancers are behind the kidnapping of Robert..."

"I don't believe you," Harper said. "I think you colluded with Professor Olsen in his despicable practices. Why don't you admit that he was your mentor? Perhaps your friend Robert even perished in one of your experiments."

"But that's not true," Julian yelled.

"ENOUGH," Harper thundered.

And before any of us could react, thick ropes flew out of his wand and wrapped themselves tightly around Ross, who, losing his balance, fell to the ground.

"Stop," I said, "deputy headmaster, I think you're making a terrible mistake. I don't think Julian is capable of..."

But Harper was maniacal and beyond reason.

"I knew it from the start!" he spat. "Amateur fools,

believing the first cock-and-bull story you hear. I warned against hiring you, and I was right all along."

Isabella shrieked with fury.

"Julian is innocent!"

And without warning, she drew her own wand. But Harper was too quick for her.

"DISPERGO," Harper cried.

Isabella Villar was lifted up and was smashed by an invisible force into the wall behind her.

Horrified, I stepped forward to confront Harper, but he pointed his wand at me.

"Not one step further, Miss Sheridan. I'm warning you. I'm taking the boy back to the castle, where he will await his lawful arrest by the MLE. Stand back, all of you. Or I will be forced to curse you."

Then, he waved his wand at the helpless Ross, whose body was lifted up from the ground and levitated through the open window, hovering ominously outside.

"If any of you follow me, I will consider it as an act of aiding a criminal and a fugitive."

He slowly backed out of the room, his wand covering all of us. Then, he vanished from sight.

CHAPTER 11

It took us a second to process what had just happened. Isabella, lying on the ground, was crying uncontrollably. Barry simply stood there, incapable of doing anything.

"Isabella," I said, kneeling next to her, "are you hurt?"

The tears still streaming down her face, she shook her head.

"What on earth just happened?" Val said shakily. "I can't believe it."

"Were you able to read Julian?" I asked. "Psychically, I mean."

"Yes, quite clearly," she said. "He was telling the truth, Amy, there was no doubt about it. He was very angry, which is understandable, of course. But it was what he saw."

"Harper," I said. "He's mad. Utterly crazy."

"H-he always hated J-Julian," Isabella said, sitting up and wiping the tears from her cheeks. "He didn't believe a word of what Julian said, just because he had played some tricks on him. But they were harmless! Nobody was ever hurt."

"Then Harper must be covering up for his own crimes," Barry said darkly. "I see no other explanation."

"He's certainly tried to sabotage our investigation from the very beginning," I said. "He tried – and failed – to convince the headmistress not to hire us. He quarrelled with her about it even after our arrival."

"That's right," said Val. "I didn't quite understand it at the time, but he felt a real loathing for Ross. You know, when we were in the headmistress's office. He wanted him expelled, remember? If it had been up to him – and not the headmistress – he would have kicked him out of the school right away."

"Could you read him?" I asked Val.

"It was very difficult," said Val. "There's a lot of boiled up resentment inside of him. But I didn't feel anything else."

"Seems to me like he's just looking for a scapegoat," I said.

"Yes," Barry said, frowning. "But we're running out of time. We're still no closer to producing any actual evidence. Let us say that Harper is our man, what do we have against him? Nothing much except for picking on the wrong person. And his bad manners. And even on the British Isles, that isn't punishable by law."

"Well, perhaps it ought to be," I said moodily. "But you're right, of course. We've got to do something. Perhaps we should approach the headmistress. Tell her what kind of a deputy she really has. She won't believe that whole story about Ross being a necromancer's apprentice and all that stuff. She said herself that Ross is just a prankster, a rascal."

"Even she won't be able to resist the authority of the MLE," said Barry. "I don't think the case looks particularly good for Ross. He's the only dot connecting one of the missing people – his friend Robert – and Professor Olsen."

"But he is innocent," Isabella said, her temper rising again.

"I realise that," Barry said. "But the law, I'm afraid, might not be in agreement. Remember that drawing the necromancer's marks is in itself already a serious offense. The more desperate the officials become, the higher the likelihood that they might try to concoct a case against him in regard to the disappearances, as well."

"That's true, Amy," said Val, turning to me. "Remember how PC Bowler tried to pin the murder on you six months ago?"

"Vividly," I said.

"A closed case," said Barry, "might be worth more to some than the truth."

"Yes," I said. "The murderer might be thinking along the same lines."

"What are you saying, Amy?" asked Val.

"I'm saying that, if I were the killer, I'd try to frame Julian Ross as quickly as possible. Plant some incriminating evidence in his room and end the entire thing. Then, they'd be free to continue their experiments without fear of repercussions."

Isabella got up. Her face was blotched and swollen from crying, though there were no tears anymore. Instead, it had been replaced by grim determination.

"We will catch this murderer," she said. "I don't care if it is Harper or someone else. Julian did what he thought was right. I didn't want him to draw those marks, but it was the only way that anyone paid attention. He wants to save his friend."

"Barry," I said. "Is there any chance that… that the disappeared people might still be alive?"

But Barry shook his head.

"I cannot say," he answered solemnly. "I am sorry, Amanda. Necromancy, well, let's say only very few people are drawn to that branch of magic. By definition, I don't think you can assume that they would behave in a normal and rational manner. If what Julian witnessed was indeed some sort of resurrection ritual through sacrifice, time is of the essence. As far as I know, it takes a long time to prepare, there is a special potion that is required, and it can easily spoil."

"Do you mean that Julian might have stopped the resurrection?" I asked.

"I think so," said Barry. "From what I understand, it is a very complicated process. The dead snakes, for instance, are a symbol of both death and healing. They play a devilish part, but don't ask me the specifics because I don't know. Without sacrifice, however, there is no resurrection. Without the potion, the resurrected will remain lifeless.

That is crucial. If the potion is not used immediately, it must be discarded and replaced by a fresh one."

"Then there might still be hope that the ritual has not been attempted again," I said.

"But how does Professor Olsen fit into all this?" asked Val.

"Well, according to Julian, he was the only one who would listen, isn't that right, Isabella?" I said.

Isabella nodded.

"Perhaps," I said. "We've been wrong about Olsen."

"What do you mean?" asked Val.

"Perhaps Olsen was *investigating* the case," I said. "That would explain why he gathered every piece of information on necromancy and Wycliffe."

"So if they silenced Olsen," Val said slowly, "he must have been close to the truth."

"Yes," I said. "Remember the red mark on the map, Barry? He must have figured out that the ritual would take place here, in the woods, thanks to Julian's account. He was sure to be on the lookout for the next ritual. Perhaps he already had his suspicions as to who was behind it all. But now that he's dead, they can go through with it."

"But we don't even know where it's taking place," said Val.

"Probably in the same place as last time," I said. "Isabella, did Julian show you the clearing with the three trees in the middle that he spoke of?"

"No," she said miserably, "he didn't. I'm sorry, I don't know where it is."

"The woods are very extensive," said Barry. "You saw it on the map. We wouldn't be able to find it in time."

"Unless," I said ponderingly, "unless we could cover the ground more quickly than on foot. Does the school have brooms?"

"Yes, of course," said Isabella, "the broom cupboards are near the East Tower."

"Right," I said. "We need three brooms, do you think you can get them without anyone noticing?"

"I think so," said Isabella.

"Good," I said. "Come to Barry's office when you've got them. We have to find that clearing."

"But what about Julian?" Isabella said. "What if the MLE gets their hands on him, or worse, the necromancer does?"

"In that regard," I said, "we'll have to take certain precautions. Val, can you go to Julian's room? We need to move his things."

"Move his things?" asked Isabella, perplexed. "But why?"

"Because you cannot plant evidence in an empty room," I said. "Val, can you take charge of that?"

"Of course, Amy," she said.

"If anyone asks, just say it's on the Earl of Barrington's authority and that Ross's things have to be moved immediately."

"Hey," said Val, "why don't we keep the room under observation? That way, if anyone tries to plant evidence, we'll know who it is."

"We could, yes," I said. "It's a long shot, though. We don't know for certain whether it will happen at all."

"I doubt they'd simply walk in," said Barry. "I suspect they'd make sure they were alone before attempting such a thing."

"Perhaps," I said, "we could ask some of the students to keep their eyes open. They wouldn't arouse suspicion in their own dormitory."

"I'll do that. But what will you do?" asked Val. "I hope you're not considering anything dangerous without us, Amy, because I won't allow it."

"No," I said, smiling. "I'll talk to the headmistress. Deputy Harper is almost certain to contact the MLE right away without letting her know. If I can get her to intervene on Ross's behalf, we can buy some time, perhaps even prevent his arrest by the MLE. At least until we have more information."

"Good thinking," said Val, nodding her head. "Just leaves our favourite aristocrat to snooze in his office."

"Actually, I could do with a nap," said Barry, groggily wiping his eyes.

"There's no time," I said. "Perhaps we can snatch a few hours later. I think we need more information on the ritual. We're still poking in the dark in regard to necromancy."

"Well," said Barry, "we'll probably remain mostly in the dark but I'll do my best. I'll get some books from the library and see what I can find out."

"Great," I said. "I'll meet you all as soon as possible in Barry's office. Isabella, you'd better tell Val where Julian's room is. And we need a spare key, too."

"It's no problem," said Isabella, "I will take care of it."

***

It was morning by the time we had returned to the castle. The lack of sleep paired with the adrenaline seemed to create a strange state akin to having drunk far too much coffee, which I had regularly done as a waitress. The seemingly endless flights of stairs I had to ascend to reach the headmistress's office didn't help, either. I'd be cursing all the way down if it turned out that she wasn't in.

I was in luck, however.

"Come," said a voice from within, after I had knocked.

Once more, I entered Muriel Hall's office. And yet, the last time almost seemed like a lifetime ago to me now. I had no time to appreciate the beauty of the desk or the view any longer. Time was our most valuable asset, and I didn't want to squander it needlessly.

"Miss Sheridan, what a pleasant surprise," she said, smiling. "I hadn't expected you back so quickly."

"Yes, well, there have been some new developments. Urgent ones, in fact."

"Oh?" she said, beckoning me to sit down on one of the chairs in front of her desk.

"Yes," I said, "you see, your deputy Mr. Harper, well, he has taken Julian Ross into custody. I think he wants to hand him over to the MLE."

"*Custody*?" she echoed, bewilderment spreading across her entire face.

"It's a long story, but suffice it to say that Julian Ross is responsible for drawing the marks of the necromancer all over the school. He's been doing it for weeks, apparently."

"Ross did that?" she said, flabbergasted. "But... but whatever for?"

"He told Mr. Harper about his suspicions that a necromancer is responsible for the abductions. I think there is good reason to believe that Ross is right about that. Mr. Harper, apparently, didn't believe him, however, and sent him away."

"I see," she said. "Very peculiar behaviour by Harper, I must say. He should have sent him straight to me with that sort of information."

"Indeed," I said. "And I'm afraid to say that he's acting independently right now, too."

"That man has been getting out of hand," she said. "But I never thought that... well, what do you suggest, Miss Sheridan?"

"In my opinion, we have to stop the MLE from arresting Ross. At least for the moment. I realise this is a big favour I'm asking, since his drawing the marks was already a criminal offense. But, you see, he might easily become a suspect – even a scapegoat – for the kidnappings. And, whatever he has done, I don't think him capable of that."

"Well," she said, "I certainly agree with that. I cannot deny that I've always had a soft spot for Ross's antics, but I cannot possibly imagine him delving into necromancy."

She took a deep breath.

"Alright, Miss Sheridan," she said. "I'll get in touch with MLE headquarters right away. If Harper has sent for them, I'll try to delay as long as possible, but I cannot promise you anything. They can be quite stubborn, you know. Especially in a case like this."

"Of course," I said. "Thank you, headmistress."

"Not at all," she said. "Where are Ross and Harper now, by the way?"

"We don't know," I said.

"I see," she said. "Well, if you happen to run into Harper, tell him that he is to report to me immediately."

"Yes, headmistress," I said.

***

Subsequently, I tried to track down Harper and Julian Ross. The likeliest place, of course, was the deputy's office. After asking several students along the way, it turned out that Harper's office was at other end of the castle, closer to the West Tower, in fact.

I wasn't really expecting to talk any sense into Harper. But at least, if he was in, I could make sure that Julian was alright. Also, I would be able to convey the headmistress's message. Seeing Harper's sneer drop from his face was reward in itself.

Perhaps it was my lack of sleep or the fact that we had traipsed through the woods for so long, but I managed to get lost twice on my way to the deputy's office. At last, however, I had found the correct corridor. The staff common room was also close by. In passing, I recognised Esther's voice from within. She seemed to be rather on edge for some reason.

Suddenly, I ran into something soft and large. It was the quarterwarlock, Mr. Armbruster.

"Sorry, Mr. Armbruster," I said, "I wasn't looking where

I was going."

"No problem," he said gruffly. "I, erm, have that list you asked for. Delivered it to the office an hour ago."

"The list?" I asked.

"Yes, with the stolen goods that went missing."

"Oh, I see. Thank you," I said. "I just need to speak to Mr. Harper right now, if you'll excuse me."

"Mr. Harper?" Mr. Armbruster said, crossing his hands in front of his belly. "Why, he's not there. Didn't answer my knock. Someone in the staff room said they saw him in the Great Hall not too long ago, though."

"OK," I said. "Thank you, I'll try there."

Mr. Armbruster shuffled down the hallway. I was just about to follow in his tracks when an idea occurred to me. There was a chance that Harper had left Julian Ross locked in his office. In any case, it wouldn't hurt if I made sure he wasn't there, I reasoned to myself. It was one place less to search for Julian later on, because I was still worried that Harper might simply take Julian and deliver him to the MLE himself if the headmistress succeeded in delaying them.

Making sure that nobody from the staff room was able to see me, I inched over to the deputy headmaster's office. The gold letters on the door were simple yet elegant. I got out my wand. Owing to past experience, I had become quite good at unlocking spells.

"Vertere," I whispered.

But nothing happened. At first I thought that the spell hadn't worked. I tried the handle, and to my surprise I found that it had already been unlocked. Gently, I pushed it open. The sight that greeted me made me hold my left hand to my mouth to stop myself from screaming.

The deputy headmaster lay sprawled across his own desk, his eyes open and unflinching. Keeping my wand at the ready, I inched forward into the room, closing the door behind me.

There could be no doubt about Harper's condition as I had seen its effects only too well in the past. He had been hit by the killing curse. There was nothing that could be done for him now.

But Julian was nowhere to be seen. The office had one more door that led to another room, however, so I tried it. And there, lying on the ground, his legs and hands still bound by heavy ropes, was Julian Ross. For one horrible moment, I thought that he, too, had been murdered. But, bending down, I noticed that Julian was still breathing, although he was unconscious. Turning around so that I could keep my eyes on the door in case the killer returned, I hastily untied Julian. He had a nasty wound at the base of his skull that was bleeding slightly. He needed medical attention immediately.

"Julian," I whispered, "Julian, you'll be alright. Tell me, who did this to you?"

With difficulty, Julian opened his eyes.

"Arm…" he murmured. "Arm…"

"What's with your arm?" I asked. "Does it hurt?"

"No," he muttered.

He pointed vaguely to the wound at the back of his head.

"Your head?"

"Arm… bruster," he breathed.

"Armbruster did this?" I said. "Are you sure?"

He nodded his head painfully.

"I can't believe it," I said.

And yet, it all seemed to make sense. As quarterwarlock, he had access to all areas of the castle. Nobody, in fact, would ever suspect him, whether he was in the dungeons or in a students' dormitory. And he most likely knew about most the secret chambers and shortcuts throughout the school.

"I've got to get you to the infirmary," I said to Julian. "As quickly as possible."

I levitated Julian out of the deputy's office and into the hall, making sure to close the door behind me again. Catching Armbruster would have to wait until Julian was in safety and taken care of.

Luckily, the staff room door was open now. As I reached it, Esther happened to come out at the exact same time. Her smile quickly faded as she saw Ross.

"What happened?" she asked. "Is he hurt?"

"Yes," I said. "It's Armbruster. He's the necromancer. We need to get Julian to the infirmary as quickly as possible. Do you know the way?"

"Why… why yes, of course. Follow me."

We turned the corner and slowly proceeded through a series of corridors I was unfamiliar with. Luckily, the infirmary wasn't too far away, and we reached it within a matter of minutes. The nurse attended to Julian immediately.

"I'll stay here with him," Esther said.

"Good," I said. "I'm sorry I can't explain everything. Please make sure that nobody sees Julian. His life may depend on it."

It was clear that Esther didn't fully understand, but she agreed to do it.

As I raced back to Barry's office, I thought only of how to trap Armbruster.

CHAPTER 12

Val and Barry were already back in the office, though Isabella hadn't returned yet with the broomsticks. I quickly filled them in on what had happened.

"Armbruster knows he doesn't have much breathing room," I said, pacing up and down in front of Barry's desk. "He must realise that it's only a matter of time before someone will discover the deputy headmaster."

"But where is he now?" asked Val.

"I don't know," I said. "He will continue with whatever he was planning, though. For once, time is against him. He has to attempt the ritual again, as soon as possible."

"I still don't understand all this necromancy business," said Val, frowning. "I mean, what are they trying to do precisely?"

"That," said Barry heavily, "is now my metier, I suppose."

"Did you find out anything?" I asked.

"Well," he said. "Not much more than Ross, I'm afraid, in regard to the ritual. But at least we could verify what he said. The ritual he described is indeed sacrificial in nature. It is designed to resurrect the dead. I went back up to the East Tower and had another look at Olsen's notes. A lot of his research is missing, that much is clear. Someone definitely searched his office."

Barry cleared his throat.

"From what I can tell, Olsen believed that the ritual could only take place at night due to the idiosyncratic effects of the potion. It spoils in sunlight, almost instantaneously. Oh, and there is one additional important factor. It appears that the act must occur at the final resting place of the dead person in question. The remains may not be moved under any circumstances, or the whole thing won't work. In other words, Armbruster must return to the clearing in the woods if he wants to successfully complete the ritual. And, as I said, it must be conducted at night, with midnight being the most potent hour."

"We still have some time," I said.

Sleep deprivation was gradually catching up with me, however. I felt dizzy and lightheaded. Confronting a dangerous necromancer, I decided, certainly required a better state of mind.

"Perhaps," I said slowly, "we should grab a few hours of sleep before we go. We'd still have more than enough time to find the clearing and get into position."

Both Barry and Val were exhausted and thus agreed to my proposal. Isabella arrived a few minutes later with the brooms under her arms. She was greatly relieved that Julian, although hurt, was in safe hands. Though she wanted to go and see him immediately, I persuaded her to take a rest, too, however short it might be. We would need all the strength for our final encounter with Armbruster that we could muster. I made myself as comfortable as I could on one of the sofas and quickly slipped into an uneasy sleep.

***

A few hours later, I awoke to the dribble of rain hitting the window panes behind me. This was a very unwelcome development, since it would make the search a lot more difficult. So, I decided we had better set off sooner rather than later.

Barry was to ride on one broom with me, while Val went with Isabella. I wanted the reserve broom just in case there were survivors or one of the brooms broke down.

You never knew when it would come in handy.

I had never flown a broom in my brief period as a witch. As I stepped out onto the window sill of Barry's office, I felt the apprehension growing within me, though Barry assured me that 'there really wasn't anything to it'. With Barry perched firmly on the handle, I hopped on. With the spare broom tied to the end, I kicked off from the ground as hard I could.

Immediately, I zoomed forward with such violence that Barry lost his grip on the handle and slipped. I grabbed his tail just in time. Howling in protest, Barry clawed his way back onto the broom.

"Careful, Amanda," he shouted. "I don't have nine lives in the air, you know."

"Sorry," I said. "Just… getting the hang of this thing."

"Well, at least we'll have the trees to break our fall, soon."

"Better than the rocks below us now," I said, looking down with a shudder.

Isabella, meanwhile, was having no trouble at all on her broom since she had enjoyed several years of school training. Val, on the other hand, looked terrified. We decided to follow the road through the woods, which was just about visible from above in spite of the rain. From there, we could branch out in each direction.

Every now and then, we'd spot a clearing, though each time the three trees in the middle were missing. The minutes and finally hours passed by without any success. The afternoon had trickled by, and we were no closer to finding Armbruster. Flying through the soft but steady downpour, I was getting ever wetter and colder.

Finally, however, the rain stopped. But the sun was beginning to set now, and a note of panic entered the equation.

"We've got to fly faster," Barry said. "Cover more

ground."

"I'm doing my best," I said. "It's just that I'm not… hold on, do you see that clearing down there?"

"We've passed that one before," Barry said dismissively.

"No, over there, on the other side."

Barry craned his neck, while still retaining his balance on the broom.

"Fly a little closer," he said.

And there, finally, was the clearing with the three trees in the middle. I hovered close to the spot, but making sure I couldn't be seen from the clearing itself, and waved my left arm at Val and Isabella.

"Have you found something?" Isabella asked as she flew next to me.

"Down there," I said. "It's the clearing alright. Three trees."

"OK," said Isabella. "So, what now?"

"We should dismount a little distance away," I said. "We don't want to advertise our arrival too much."

"Yeah," said Val, looking down. "Also, the sooner we get off these things, the better."

Isabella and I both began our descent about a hundred yards away, carefully gliding between the treetops. We landed softly and relatively quietly, if you discounted Val's muffled cry as she hit her toe on a tree trunk.

With only a few yards left to the clearing, we hid our brooms beneath some leaves and waited for Armbruster to appear.

We stood there, waiting as the sun bathed the surrounding trees in a deep red and eventually disappeared entirely. But the darkness that enveloped us also gave us superior cover. Midnight was not too far away now.

And finally, a light appeared at the other side of the clearing. Then, a hooded figure emerged from the trees, a wand in one hand and a body slung over its shoulder.

Though hooded, dressed in the same black robe that Julian Ross had described earlier, there was no doubt in my mind that this had to be Armbruster, as the gait and size matched his perfectly.

After Armbruster had placed the body on the altar, he lit several torches, placing them in their brackets. Then, he raised his wand, slowly pointing it at each of the three large trees in succession. As he did so, he began to chant a mysterious spell, the words of which I didn't recognise.

"We'd better move," I said.

I quietly signalled to Isabella, the only other person in our party with a wand, to prepare our attack. We had decided that we would approach him from a slight angle, though not wide enough that our spells might threaten to hit one another. Armbruster would be forced to concentrate his fire on one of us, giving the other a decisive advantage.

Val and Barry were to stay in the background until the coast was clear, as they were both unarmed.

Slowly, we inched forward. We had reached the edge of the clearing, and Armbruster still seemed impervious to our approach. Still chanting, he had his back turned to us, evidently preoccupied with preparations for the ritual.

It was probably the most favourable opportunity we'd get. Once more, I gave Isabella a sign. Swiftly, we covered the yards of open ground. Armbruster still had his back turned to us.

"Stop what you're doing immediately, Armbruster," I said loudly, making sure that I kept him covered with my wand.

The cloaked man spun round to face us. Though his hood hid his face, I recognised his voice.

"You," Armbruster hissed. "What are you doing here?"

"I might ask you the same thing," I said.

"You would never understand," he said. "Nobody does.

117

Necromancy is a fine art, once mastered. But it is not for those who are weak or faint at heart."

"This madness ends here, Armbruster," I said.

"Ah, but it won't," he said. "It is only the beginning."

"What are you talking about?" I said.

"It is all as planned," he said, stroking the altar. "And you will not stop me."

Then, Armbruster rolled behind the altar with a nimbleness that I would never have suspected of him. Both Isabella and I fired hexes but missed. Now, Armbruster was using the person lying on the altar as a shield. We held our fire.

Yet Armbruster had no such restrictions. He immediately started pelting us with spell after spell. I dashed forward, seeking refuge behind one of the massive trees, while Isabella gave me cover.

Meanwhile, Barry and Val were nowhere to be seen. I had rapidly lost control of the entire situation. Isabella, under fire from Armbruster, was forced to retreat behind a small rock formation, only a few inches high. He had her pinned down. I tried to step out from behind the tree, but Armbruster's reactions were too fast, with one spell missing me by no more than an inch. Now, he had both of us bogged down.

At least, I thought, the ritual had been stopped for the time being. And yet, I could only direct a hex at him when Armbruster tried to stray too far away from the altar. We were, effectively, caught in a stalemate.

And then, I heard a rushing sound from above. My eyes tore upwards, and I saw that Val was flying on a broom – with Barry sitting on the handle – shooting like an arrow straight for Armbruster and the altar. Just as he spotted them in the air, I dashed out from behind the tree and charged.

Val dived low; too low, for she painfully grazed the edge

of the altar with her foot, pelting her body towards Armbruster like a cannonball. Armbruster dodged just in time, but it provided Barry with enough time to jump right on top of him, slashing viciously at him with his claws. I didn't dare shoot a spell for fear of hitting Barry, so I lunged forward, ramming my entire body as hard as I could against Armbruster. Trying to fight both of us off at the same time, he lost his balance and collapsed to the ground in front of the altar, and his wand went flying high through the air.

Isabella, who had also joined the fight, caught it neatly with her left hand.

Scrambling to our feet, we now had Armbruster defenceless and cornered.

"It's over Armbruster," I said, panting, my wand now pointed at his massive chest. "The game's up."

Fear and hatred etched across his face, he stared at me, though there was nothing he could do. Conjuring up ropes with my wand, I made them wrap themselves around Armbruster's body, rendering him harmless. Then, I hurried across to Val, who was lying on the ground and nursing her leg.

"Val," I said, bending down, "what's wrong?"

"It's my ankle," she said, her face contorted in pain. "It's broken. I can't... it hurts so much."

"We've got to get you to the infirmary," I said. "Isabella, give me a hand, will you?"

Together, we lifted Val up. But she wasn't going anywhere with that ankle of hers. She needed immediate help. I quickly retrieved our brooms from their hiding places and brought them into the clearing.

"Isabella," I said. "Please take Val to the infirmary. Julian is also there. I'm sure he'll be pleased to see you."

"And I him," she said, beaming. "We solved it."

"Yes," I said. "We did."

119

"Will you be alright with Armbruster?" she asked, stretching out the wand she had caught and handing it to me.

"Yes," I said, tucking Armbruster's wand into my back pocket. "It's fine. He's all tied up. We can have the MLE pick him up later. Tell the headmistress to get them here as quickly as possible."

"OK," Isabella said, getting onto her broom. "I will tell her."

I helped Val get on behind her. Then, Isabella kicked off from the ground. Within a minute, they were out of sight.

CHAPTER 13

Exhausted but pleased that we had been able to thwart Armbruster's plans, I walked over to him, making sure that he was still bound tightly. He lay there, next to the altar, furiously staring ahead of him into the darkness. He would pose no threat.

Above him, the figure on the altar remained perfectly still. It also wore a cloak and a hood.

"Do you recognise who it is?" I asked Barry.

He leapt nimbly onto the altar.

"It looks like a woman's figure," he said slowly.

I stepped closer to the large stone. Slowly, I lifted the hood covering the woman's face. To my shock, it was the headmistress, Muriel Hall. Her eyes were closed.

"Is she... dead?" asked Barry.

I looked at her face. It was perfectly motionless.

Then, without warning, her eyes suddenly tore wide open. I yelled, almost losing my balance, stumbling backwards.

Muriel Hall reacted like lightning. With a flick of her own wand, she had mine fly right into her open palm. Before I could anything, thin cords of steel shot out of her wand, binding my hands and legs tightly together, so that I keeled over onto the ground like a log. Then, she cast a torrent of freezing curses, directed at Barry. He desperately scampered across the clearing, running towards the three trees for cover, but one of the many spells finally made contact with him. At once, his entire body was encased in a block of ice.

"Miss Sheridan," the headmistress said, a triumphant smile on her face. "You don't think I'd let poor old Armbruster deal with you all on his own, did you? I must say, it was rather kind of you to send your friends away. That makes it a lot easier for me."

"But…" I spluttered, "but how could it be *you*? You hired us in the first place."

"Ah," she said. "That is indeed an interesting question. You see, I had no choice but to hire you, Miss Sheridan. The school board wasn't happy at all with the work the MLE had done. Especially Professor Olsen. He and the *Spellcasting Parents' Association* demanded an independent investigation, so I had to pretend to go along with it, fashioning it as my own idea. I played my role as the overworked and pathetic headmistress of Warklesby's School of Magic, who couldn't even control her own deputy, dutifully."

My head was still spinning, the shock and betrayal only just sinking in.

"You killed Professor Olsen," I said. "And then you staged it as a suicide."

"Quite right, Miss Sheridan," she said, without a hint of remorse. "You see, he was unsatisfied with the MLE investigation and promptly decided to start his own meddling. I am afraid to say that he got rather close to the truth. So I disposed of him, cloaking it as a suicide."

"But… why…?" I stammered.

"Well, my dear, it is a long and fascinating story. Should I tell you how Wycliffe and I became lovers in my senior year? Or how we planned his deeds together, meticulously to the last detail? Or how he went to prison for the witch he loved? Yes, I would like to chat about all that, Miss Sheridan. And I am sure it would be of the greatest interest to you, but I'm afraid I will have to cut the history lesson short."

"You were Wycliffe's accomplice all along," I breathed.

"Oh, much more than that," she said. "He called me his pupil. I learned from the master, you see, the great and noble art of necromancy. An art that spellcasters everywhere have chosen to abandon out of weakness."

"Look where your *noble* art got you," I said, disgusted, "look where it got Wycliffe. A prison cell for life. And then death."

"Yes, I admit that fate had struck a harsh blow," the headmistress said with a rueful smile. "I couldn't save him from it, although I tried many times. The prison was too well protected, you see. There was never any way of getting him out of there alive. So, I thought one day, his freedom was only possible through death."

"What are you talking about?" I said. "What good would that…"

"Oh, more than you think, Miss Sheridan. After his death, I recommended a nice and quiet spot where we could put his remains in an anonymous grave, here in the woods near the school. Nobody would ever know. Except for me, of course. And the government, being the fools that they are, were glad to be rid of the problem of his final resting place."

"But Ross disturbed your plans," I said.

"Yes," she said, "that was an unfortunate setback. It took months to concoct the potion again, but now I am ready – ready to resurrect the great Wycliffe!"

With horror, I saw Muriel Hall flourish her wand again, now pointing it at Armbruster. She levitated his body over the altar and set him down upon it.

"Headmistress," he began, panic in his every syllable. "Please don't, I…"

But Muriel Hall silenced him with a wave of her wand.

"Yes, poor Armbruster," she said, a merciless smile on her face. "You see, Miss Sheridan, he never quite understood the role he was to play in this. For Wycliffe to walk among us again, I am afraid that certain sacrifices have to be made. Goodbye, faithful Armbruster."

Without hesitation, she cast the killing curse. A jet of red light hit Armbruster square in the chest. He was dead.

Horrified, I looked around for anything that could help me escape my bindings. And then, I remembered Armbruster's own wand that I had pocketed earlier. But my hands were bound behind my back, and so I couldn't quite reach it, no matter how hard I tried.

"Miss Sheridan, you have witnessed the death of a servant," she screamed. "And now, I want you to witness the rebirth of a genius."

She directed her wand at the ground in front of her and began to chant. It was the most terrifying sound I had ever heard, like a sinister song that never stopped. It was a calling that only the dead could answer. And before long, I was sure they would.

I sat up straight, trying to change the angle of the wand in my pocket. As the song got louder, my fingertips were already grasping at the wand, but I couldn't quite take it.

Meanwhile, to my horror, the earth was loosening in the place at which Muriel Hall was pointing. Her spell was finally working. Time was running out before Wycliffe would walk amongst the living once more.

With one desperate jerk, I finally grabbed the wand in my hand.

"Libero!" I cried, pointing the wand at my own bindings, which fell to the ground immediately.

Muriel Hall tore her wand away from the ground, readying for the attack, but she was too slow for my own.

"ABIGO," I yelled.

A jet of white light emitted from the end of my wand. Muriel Hall was propelled backwards, flying through the air. With a deafening crack, the back of her head connected with the nearest tree trunk. Unconscious, she slid to the ground.

To my amazement, the tree began to tremble, shaking precariously from side to side. Barry, still frozen within his prison of ice, was within range if the tree was to fall in his direction.

Without another thought, I leapt over to him, kicking the block of ice encasing Barry to safety. I was just about to run when a crack appeared in the centre of the trunk. It was widening. Transfixed, I couldn't move an inch, for within the trunk, the sleeping face of a youth – no older than sixteen, perhaps – appeared.

CHAPTER 14

A week later, we were all back safely at Fickleton House, tucking in to an excellent cooked breakfast made by Mrs. Faversham. We had put Val's foot, now in a thick plaster, on a small footstool. She still needed crutches to get around the house but the medical warlock had assured us that there wouldn't be any permanent damage, and that the healing potion would eventually fix all of the broken bones in her ankle.

Atop his high chair, which had been adapted to his feline needs, including a cat ladder and holsters for his bowl and drinks, Barry was wrapped in a green and red tartan blanket. He was wearing a pained expression as he slurped the remainders of the chicken soup that Mrs. Faversham had made specially for him.

After the events in the clearing, Muriel Hall had been arrested by the MLE and charged with multiple counts of abduction, murder, and necromancy. Though the trial was still due to begin, she was most likely going to spend the rest of her life as her lover and mentor, Wycliffe, had done: in prison.

"I'm surprised that cold of yours hasn't cleared up yet, Barry," I said, with a wink in Val's direction.

"Well, he was in that ice cube for quite some time, you know," said Val, grinning. "It will take a lot of chicken soups to warm up after that one."

"Mock me all you like," Barry said, in what he thought to be a dignified voice, "but I'd like to see *you* after such a horrendous experience. I could have easily died. Especially after Amanda kicked me across half the clearing like a football."

"I told you, Barry," I said, "there was no time to carry

you. I was afraid that the tree was going to fall on top of you. You wouldn't have wanted that, would you?"

"It was quite obvious that the tree was not in the process of falling," Barry said sniffily.

"But what *exactly* happened there, anyway?" asked Val, "I still don't understand why they had kept the boy in that tree."

"It was part of the ritual," I said. "The MLE examined it later – that was while Barry was being unfrozen and you were being treated in the infirmary, Val. After I got Barry out of there, I called for the MLE and showed them the clearing. We found the other abducted people in the other two trees."

"I get that, Amy," said Val, "but why did they do it in the first place?"

"Well," I said, "after Wycliffe's return, they were to be used in the second step of the resurrection. After sacrificing Armbruster, Wycliffe would have just been a walking shell, a body without a mind. But if Muriel Hall had succeeded, sacrificing the other three and then administered the potion, he would have regained his old strength, perhaps even rising to greater power than ever before."

"Do you really think that plan would have worked?" asked Val. "Or was the headmistress just crazy?"

"I don't know," I said. "The MLE certainly seemed to take it very seriously."

"Lucky we got there in time, then," said Val. "Were they still alive? The people they had kidnapped, I mean."

"Eventually, yes," I said. "They had been put in a form of magical stasis. But it was for far too long, so they had trouble restoring them back to normal. I think one of the teachers got them back in the end. You should have seen the look on Julian's face when his best friend walked into the Great Hall later that day. He thought for certain that he'd be dead."

"Good thing that Julian wasn't charged," said Val.

Much to the delight of Isabella Villar, my recommendation in front of a preliminary court hearing held at the school, during which I had requested leniency for Julian Ross, had been granted. In light of the vital role he had played in solving the case, I thought that was the least we could do for him.

"Yep," I said, "he didn't even get a reprimand from the school. So all's well."

At that moment, Barry began coughing violently.

"Poor Barry," said Val sympathetically.

"Yes," I said, grinning. "But don't worry, Barry, we'll look after you."

"I think," he said, holding his paw to his throat, "it will be a very long time – perhaps even months – before this clears up. My body just isn't as strong as it used to be, you know. Also, I doubt my fur will ever look the same again."

"Sounds like you need a rest, Barry," said Val fondly, while I was trying not to laugh.

"Funny you should mention that," he continued, pointing to a stack of envelopes on the sideboard behind me. "I think you'd better see what came in the morning post, Amanda. I would get it myself, but in my present condition… I believe it's *very* important."

"Oh no," I groaned. "Not all over again. If it's from Warklesby's, I'm not going to open it."

"Amanda," said Barry, "I don't think this can wait. It's of the utmost importance."

Reluctantly, I walked over to the sideboard and picked up the stack of letters. Most of them were bills, including the repairs to Barry's library, which had gone smoothly thanks to Mrs. Faversham's supervision.

Taking my seat at the table again, I filed through the bills until I reached a mysterious blue envelope, which was addressed in a curly yet neat handwriting.

"What does it say, Amy?" Val asked.

My curiosity mixing with a strange sense of foreboding,

I tore it open and began to read aloud:

Dear Amanda Sheridan,

Thank you very much for your interest in the Magical Holiday Retreat! Please find enclosed a brochure with all the exciting activities, luxurious rooms, and wonderful relaxation our establishment has to offer. Children and pets are very welcome.

Yours sincerely,
Archibald Pomeroy

"*Magical Holiday Retreat*? Seriously, Barry?" I said. "What a build-up. You really missed your calling as an actor, you know."

Barry looked rather pleased with himself.

"But this looks amazing," said Val, who was reading the brochure more closely, "Look, Amy, it's got an elemental sauna, a bar, magic fireplace with randomised fireworks…"

"Oh no, not you, too, Val," I said.

"It's possibly the best retreat for warlocks and witches in the country," Barry said.

"It's not the kind of holiday involving sorcerers again like last time, is it?" I asked.

"Certainly not," said Barry. "Whatever gave you that idea?"

*****

Amy, Val, and Barry return in BLIND CAT'S HOLIDAY, the fourth part in the series, available on Amazon (click here).

For even more of Barry, receive a discount for books 1 – 5 in the COZY CONUNDRUMS COLLECTION, available now on Amazon (click here).

AUTHOR'S NOTE

Thank you for reading COPYCAT MURDERS. I hope you enjoyed reading it as much as I did writing it!

To spread the word, please consider leaving a review on Amazon by clicking here and on Goodreads by clicking here. It's a great way of supporting the series. A quick note that you liked it really goes a long way and is deeply appreciated.

I'll see you in the next adventure!

Yours truly,
T.H. Hunter

DEDICATION

To my beloved spouse, who believed in me from the start.

Printed in Great Britain
by Amazon